ECHO YEAR

CASPER SILK

Pale Fire Press

First Print Edition

Library of Congress Control Number: 2013900192

ISBN: 978-0-9838612-4-9

Echo Year Online: http://palefirepress.com

For information about subsidiary rights, bulk purchases or author events, contact biz@palefirepress.com.

To the David Crowns of the
world, who recognize their
own puniness but do the
impossible anyway

For my readers

From *Souvenirs Entomologiques*
Jean-Henri Fabré

Lionel Passes the Empty Chateau

The Crown chateau sold last week to a Spanish horse breeder, old money, who intends to hide his mistress there. A pair of Paso Finos have preceded her, tethered on the summit where David Crown once planted a pair of date palms—gone now. From a distance the horses appear mythical, fiery, yet their presence gives no pleasure. Already the Spaniard's peons have begun construction on the stables.

Lionel Olivier has seen a hundred foreigners come and go from Beautemps, hurling forget-me-nots and curses, their trash bins heaped with imported whiskey. Their names escape him—all but David's. The one memorable character, both by nature and circumstance.

It is customary for new arrivals to pay a visit to the mayor's office, so he was not surprised when David Crown appeared there one afternoon in early April. The Englishman presented himself at the *mairie* wearing a clean, ironed shirt and polished shoes; an act unremarkable in itself, yet in contrast to the average drop-in a seal of distinction. Lionel's expectations of new residents have contracted in recent years. They might have money, as evidenced in the ambitious renovations they undertake and fortunes they sink in hot tubs and lap pools, but their taste tends increasingly toward kitsch, their etiquette toward anarchy. Amid this mass devolution, David arrived in Beautemps and purchased its finest remaining *grande maison*.

I wanted to introduce myself, Monsieur Olivier—am I intruding?"

"*Pas du tout.*" Lionel had, in fact, been about to leave for home. After a proper handshake and exchange of bona fides, "So you have bought the widow Dampierre's domaine. I suppose the estate agent told you it was a Mansard?"

"Why yes—"

"A lie. Don't let the roof mislead you. The house was built in 1722 by the Duke's heir, the Duke having died abroad of the *mal Anglais*. True, it was spared the frills of rococo but look closely at the façade. The stones aren't from here. Beautemps' own quarry had been depleted by then; the stones had to have been hauled in on mule-back. They have a golden cast."

"I thought it was the light."

"No, *monsieur*, the stone itself is *dorée*. You have been marked."

The Englishman, visibly delighted by the revelation, nonetheless deflected its glory. "Marked for a spell of hard work. The interior is in ruins."

"The house does have character," Lionel had to concur. "You will wish to change its name, I suppose?"

"I didn't know it had one."

"It has always been called the *Vie Dorée*."

"The golden life," the newcomer translated with a sort

of reverence. "No, I shan't change the name. The *Vie Dorée* it stays."

"It will be a summer residence?" A forgone conclusion. The village's foreign population fled each autumn at the first sign of frost, except for one oddball, a farmer (something David clearly was not).

"Actually, I plan to live in Beautemps year-round, to settle here."

"You are retired then?"

Once again David had surprised him. "Work will take some sorting out. First, the house. The restoration will absorb me for some time. I'm committed to keeping the details authentic. I want to see the chateau come alive."

And then Lionel surprised himself, "Do you play chess?"

The games quickly became part of his routine—he looked forward to them—and David Crown became a frequent guest, crafty at the board, amusing over a pastis, and popular with his wife, who saw in the Englishman's mildness and sense of duty the underpinnings of chivalry.

A Day in the Life of David Crown

Summer's brink. David awoke to a morning heady with apricot blossoms and new desire. Church bells syncopated, out of time. Time itself out of time. To awaken in such a place was to commune with something large, lifting; practicalities were the furthest thing from his mind. All thought, in fact, had fled. He reached out a hand and ran it pulsing through corkscrew strands of golden hair—hers. Rowena, a woman young enough to look dewy at 6 a.m. She preened in her sleep and the back of her hand skimmed along the duvet, lowering it, revealing the precipitous rise of a breast. His eyes traced the contour upward to where her nipple pointed with an organic *hauteur* toward the vaulted ceiling, newly plastered and painted in Renaissance tones; the whole of the room suddenly an extension of her flesh—cornices, mantel, even the walls, subtly convex and the color of crème fraiche.

There was time enough before breakfast. He could hear Madame Fermat's vintage moped sputter up the graveled driveway; in a moment the housekeeper would let herself in the rear door, tie on her chintz apron, and prime the coffee mill. David's mother, Miriam, would pad down the stairs in her feathered mules and the two would begin their daily jousting—but there was time. Rationing breath he inched aside the duvet and cupped the small of Rowena's back.

A second awakening to the buzz of an egg timer. The sun climbed higher in the window frame; starlings swept past; a rosebud opened. Rowena's breath, tinged with clove, played at the edges of his cheek stubble. Too soon he heard Miriam's mules click-clack against the marble stairs. Too soon his lover's body reasserted its separateness, leaving the room's angles and arches a mere contrivance of architecture. He hefted his torso onto an elbow, scissored free his legs. The aroma of brewing coffee heralded breakfast.

"Let's not go down," Rowena said, shadowing him to the tub, loitering there in a haze of steam.

"Have to. Miriam is already at loggerheads with Madame Fermat. Can't afford to lose another housekeeper."

She dangled a hand in the current of bathwater. "You go," she said and retraced her steps to the bed, where she wrestled a moment with the snarl of linen before perching to pull on a pair of boxers. He stifled an urge to tug them down again.

"Once things are in order here, we'll get away."

Standing up, flashing him one of her *yeah-right* smiles, she twanged the waistband onto her hips.

Twenty minutes later, freshly bathed, the aftershave prickling his cheeks, David left her at the bedroom door. "There's something I need to scout in the city."

"What is it this time?"

"Gargoyles." These were lately making a comeback in the village, spurred by the influx of well-heeled northerners intent on salvaging the village's decaying medieval quarter. "A pair of them for those two gaps in the parapet." Actually, he quite liked the house as it was, as he had made it, but once the renovation was complete, what other occupation did he have? One had to be found. He would find it—eventually. "I'll tell mother you're catching up on your sleep."

"A topping idea," she said, attempting to imitate his London accent but sounding instead like a stand-in for Eliza Doolittle.

David descended the stairs with his head lowered, tracing the loping gray veins in the native red marble and making a mental note to look into runners. At the bottom he turned left, crossed a stately foyer (true to the estate agent's description), and entered the kitchen, where his mother presided over a table of empty chairs. Madame Fermat, her back turned, called from the stove, "I suppose you'll complain that the coffee is bitter. It has been sitting in the urn for an hour."

"Just the way I fancy it," he replied, dipping at the knee to survey his mother's expression.

"One mustn't look too closely at a woman first thing in the morning, kinder to wait. Where's Rowena?"

"Resting. The adjustment."

"It's been—three weeks, more? You'd think after three weeks..." His mother's lower lip rose to subsume the upper. "Rather like living with a ghost, isn't it? We hear her rattling about but never see her."

The housekeeper set down a cup and saucer, gestured

with a flourish toward the sugar bowl. "Your coffee. The fruit scones I cannot answer for. Your mother forced her recipe upon me." She pinced the doughy clods between thumb and index finger. "Lead *pelotes*."

"What is she saying?" Miriam's face colored behind its film of pancake make-up. "If it's about the scones…"

David's boarding school French sufficed for only the most pat transactions, and he could not be certain he had understood the housekeeper. "Madame Fermat comes recommended by the mayor himself."

"They have their ways."

Alert to the least change of demeanor, he glanced at the spry Alsatian who could not have been much younger than Miriam herself. "Can't be helped. We're not in England, after all."

"Mrs. Rhodes has an English girl—well, not English exactly, but English-speaking. Bosnian then."

"That's Hedy Rhodes, but we're more sporting. When in Rome…"

"She was looking for you yesterday. Something about gargoyles."

What was it about these dreadful figures leering down from their perches with maws dripping runoff that made them every newcomer's must-have?

The housekeeper, hovering midway between the table and oven with an air of condescension, wiped her palms on the starched flanks of her apron. Translucent puffs of flour blotted her wake. "More butter, more jam… cream for your peaches? But how bony you all are."

"*Merci, madame.* Bit of a hurry." Then for Miriam's benefit, "Errands to run in the city."

Taking a last swallow of tepid coffee, he pushed back his chair.

"Shall I expect you for tea?"

"Depends." On traffic, on finding the reclamation yard; the world beyond Beautemps posed a welter of challenges large and small. "Don't wait for me."

His mother removed the napkin from her lap and replaced it in its silver ring. "I'll look in on Rowena for you," she volunteered, already angling her cheek for a kiss.

David pecked the wrinkled jowl and made for the door, where a morning the color of cornflowers soothed away all qualms. The air, fresh as only country air can be, still held a nip. He couldn't resist running a hand along the chateau's façade, the stone worn smooth and etched by time's passage with a cryptic narrative. Easing the Volvo estate car from the garage, winding down the freshly graded driveway, he glanced back toward the bedroom window; no sight of Rowena, yet his heart quickened just the same.

He drove without haste. Up north he had lived breathlessly, blindly—had not lived, had only kept appointments. In Beautemps the roads curved, gates opened onto courtyards, conversation spilled into the streets. Often he would catch sight of the Dutch farmer obsessed with the notion of cultivating truffles, out tending his oaks and hazelnuts. Alongside, festooned in trellised vines and faux medieval statuary, *Maison Joyeuse*, home of Hedy and Cecil Rhodes. Farther on, a cobbled square (more triangular than square) marked the village's center, bounded by the town hall, the charcuterie, which with a pair of tables in front doubled as the village's sole bistro, and a flat denuded swath of park where old-timers played boules. Widows draped like plaster saints in the lace curtains that dissembled their vigil spied at balconies along his route. In front of the war memorial a street cleaner, garlic cloves filling the empty spaces where his teeth had once been, forever polished the bronze belly of the imperious Marianne.

The church bell struck nine. Fifty-seven seconds later

the clock atop the *mairie*, louder, if less resonant, tolled nine again. For as long as people could remember it had been this way: time colliding with itself, history held hostage, seconds, minutes, hours trundling rusted from a faulty mechanism.

On the village's far flank Lionel Olivier, a weathered yachting cap shading his eyes from the morning sun, padded along the dirt path toward the *Rivière Rieux*, so-named for the raucous peals of wind and running water that issue from the gorge through which it flows. He carried a can of spar varnish in his right hand and in the left a thick boar-bristle brush. He was whistling—not the melodic whistle that mimics music but the sound a reed might make in harmony with the river itself. Lionel seemed as much a part of the landscape as the dust he raised. As David cruised past he looked up, set down his tin can, and lifted his cap in a silent Godspeed.

There is only one road out of Beautemps, a narrow asphalt ribbon edged by mulberry trees that form a bower above it; until one reaches the windmill, where it hairpins and the shoulder falls away. At that spot, off to the left, stand three crosses, one holding the agonizing body of a crucified Christ. The sight of it never failed to slow the breath through David's windpipe, then the road would widen, and exhaling, switching on the radio, he settled back to enjoy the drive.

The countryside surrounding Beautemps sprawled myriad shades of green and gold and melted into a horizon so gossamer it might have been a mirage. Vineyards predominated, but it was the sunflowers that drew the eye with their rapt, upturned faces. Goats pastured the fallow patches, bells tinkling at their necks. Not yet patterned by the region's geometries, David let his gaze scavenge the roadsides. Gradually, almost imperceptibly, the hills subsided and a network of highways spread its tentacles through an otherwise verdant plain. Landscape gave way to cityscape, and the traffic around him tightened to a knot.

David had no difficulty following the directions Hedy had given him. The reclamation yard lay on the city's edge, visible from the highway. An eyesore but also a trove of salvaged artifacts tracing the evolution—arguably, devolution—of modern taste: Doric columns, stone fonts, brass altar rails, slabs of slate and bitumen felt, sundials, weathercocks, toilets, barbed wire…

He took the precaution of locking the car door. The parking lot lay empty and the neighborhood beyond it, derelict, fanned out in a web of narrow streets where people walked with their shoulders curled forward. As he crossed the pavement a young man in a windbreaker and dark glasses approached with a Gauloise clamped between his lips, asking for a light. David had given up smoking years ago and carried no matches. There was only the car lighter, so he doubled back and the stranger followed. A moment's pause as the coil turned a torrid orange then the young man in black positioned his cigarette, took an audible drag, glanced up— the lenses of his shades cast back a reflection of chain-link fencing. If there were eyes behind the glass, David couldn't see them, yet he felt himself scrutinized. He foraged his meager repertoire of French colloquialisms for appropriate chitchat but the stranger, abruptly veering, walked off.

"My pleasure." A reflex, lost on the man's receding back.

David replaced the lighter, relocked the car door. A sign at the yard's entrance cautioned, *"Vous le cassez, vous l'a acheté."* Taking care to pin his elbows tight against his ribs, he entered the jumble of random treasures: ballast, Belgian trusses, wickets, angel beams, choir screens, urinals, mousetraps… And then he saw them, the perfect gargoyles: two bulldog-faced monks dozing over their hymnals. A matched pair. Elated to have fulfilled his quest, eager to head home, he hefted his purchases onto a rusty trolley, took the wallet from his trouser pocket, and hurried toward a makeshift checkout.

"Ah, the sleeping monks," said the attendant, looking up from an annotated racing sheet. "You have seen the inscription in their books?"

Covering his oversight David read aloud, "*Vis a tergo*?" Never good at Latin, he could only guess at its meaning. "What do you make of it?"

"You are talking to a rationalist, *monsieur*. If you ask me, the only monk with anything to say was Rabelais."

"But what sort of water spout would he have made?"

David's French didn't suffice to convey the remark's wit, and his interlocutor gave him a look—by then familiar—not so much bewildered as resigned. He vowed, for the umpteenth time, to refresh his syntax.

Ten minutes later, with the monks snugly stowed into the back of his Volvo, he decided to head into town. A quick stop at the library and he would still make it home in time for tea. Not familiar with the neighborhood, he took a roadmap from the glove compartment. A shaft of sunlight illumined the cartographer's red and black and blue squiggles. The day had turned humid. He was about to refold the map when a shadow fell on it, engulfing the eastern seaboard, spilling into the Atlantic. Storm clouds? He poked his head out the door to glance up at the sky: mist. Rain, if it came, would come slowly.

The library lay at the heart of the business district. He parked at a distance and wove through throngs of shoppers and street vendors. Their very numbers kept him moving. At an unfamiliar corner he paused to read a street sign, and noticed beyond it a high wrought iron gate bearing an ornate plaque: *Synagogue Bet Shalom, 1837.*

His hand rose of its own volition to touch the raised

lettering, to follow its curving trajectory the way a blind man reads Braille. The building, its stone façade weathered, its doors wide and windows tall, was not an impressive piece of architecture by any means but coherent, solid. He tried the gate and found it locked. He took a few steps in one direction then the other, thinking there might be another entrance. An alleyway, narrow as a gutter, flanked the far side and along its length he edged. Spotting an opening in the iron bars, he slipped inside.

Only to discover he was not alone. A teenage boy in a motorcycle helmet and cropped pants paced nearby, smoking inside a partially lifted visor.

Not in the habit of trespassing, David had no stock excuse for his presence there. Needing to say something, he ventured a feeble, *"Un édifice malchanceux, non?"* and motioned toward the building's pocked and faded façade.

The boy flicked away his cigarette, snapped down his visor.

Feeling decidedly unwelcome David excused myself, dipped his left shoulder, and tried to sidle back through the railing—froze in this posture, feeling the nape of his neck burn cold. A sudden yank at his shirt collar sent him tumbling on the diagonal, landing on his feet but staggering heel-over-toe without control. A body broke his momentum, or more specifically a foot. He felt its tire-tread sole thump him on the coccyx, sending him careening forward. He barely had time to cry "Hey!" when a hand grabbed him by the throat.

There were two of them then, or was David seeing double? *"Juif,"* the taller of his assailants pronounced.

Grappling for balance, David stole a glance at the young man. Although his forehead glistened with sweat, he still wore the same black windbreaker. "First at the salvage yard, now here... what do you want with me? A mistake, there's been a mistake."

Assailant number two, acne-faced behind his visor, jabbed an elbow into David's side. *"Juif,"* came the muffled echo.

David's first thought was, they want my wallet; better to give it to them than take a beating. He reached for his trouser pocket, but the man in the windbreaker caught hold of his wrist and wrenched it.

"Just tell me what you want—money? Passport?"

The moto boy mimicked him: *"Argent? Passeport?"*

"But I'm English. I'm English." David tapped his chest with an index finger. "English." As in punting on the Thames, fair play, cucumber sandwiches. Tap, tap. "I'm English, damn it!"

"Anglais, Inglis..." Tap, tap.

"Zioniste!" hissed number one, to which his brother-in-arms added, *"Feuj!"*

"You don't understand, I'm English. An Englishman, full stop."

"Inglis." Tap.

Whatever David said seemed only to provoke the reaction least desired—a jab, an escalation of abuse. Reason was no defense at all. He tried again to extract his wallet. "Money?"

"Argent?"

Able no longer to contain himself, David barreled into number two, if only to open an escape route. Fumbling for his visor, cursing, the boy crumpled to his knees. He was still cursing as David leapfrogged him and scrabbled toward the gate.

But the man in the windbreaker caught up with David, kicked his feet out from under, and brought him down. His sunglasses dangled from one ear. David searched for his eyes but saw only the black fire of hatred. *"Feelty* Jew!" he screamed in a whisper, and a fist breached David's foundering defenses, swelled to the size of a juggernaut, then vanished in a red fog.

◆

A house in France. A lover. Time. The dream had been with him since adolescence, a modest and unoriginal whim yet enduring. Others leave their dreams unfulfilled for lack of opportunity or cash, but David, having been born a Crown, reluctant scion of a growing electronics chain, could hardly plead poverty. On what, then, to pin his years of inaction? Half a century and he has not made a mark, unless one counts the trim gray groove of the dutiful man.

And perhaps poverty may have suited him better. The family business, though it kept him in gadgets, also bound him to a desk, a payroll, and the dreary London suburb that engulfed its headquarters. It all began with the number-eight torch battery. David's father, known to the buying public as Willy for Wireless, sold them in his radio repair shop, a sideline—until the war broke with its blackouts and air raids. What wouldn't a person pay for a beam of light in a darkness so complete it devoured nations? Willy's fortune was made.

When David thinks of his father now, as he often does, he sees a man propped in a hospital bed with tubes up his nose and a telephone in each hand, saying, "You think it's easy?" Had Willy's heart held, he might have lit up the world.

The business outlived him, passing upon his death to his two sons. Barry, older by ten years, battle-scarred from birth, assumed the helm, as he had been groomed to do. David, never suited to commerce, sat captive in an office, fielding lawsuits. Only last year, when a multinational forced its way in, did Barry finally release him. He was forty-nine years old, divorced, and working on an ulcer. It was time to begin.

◆

When David next opened his eyes, flames filled them. From where he lay the synagogue seemed to be breathing fire. The smell of petrol made him hack. Thinking of nothing but his next breath, he staggered to his feet. His right cheek throbbed, the whole of his right side. The rest was numbness.

There was no one in sight, only an eerie orange glow, only the silver-white plumes of smoke that billowed from the windows. It occurred to him that someone may still have been inside the building, trapped, overcome by smoke. Shielding his eyes he raced forward, glass shards crackling beneath his soles, sirens wailing in the distance, and an image locked away somewhere between heart and gut: himself as a young man, entering a synagogue not so different from this one. Himself and yet not, but that was another story. More moth than man he made for the blaze.

And then David saw him: a gnome-like figure, bearded and plump, cradling a smoldering bundle of something, teetering forward with it. Framed in fire he appeared indestructible, imbued by the gods with ribs of asbestos and an iron aura the flames could not penetrate. *"Voyez-vous, monsieur?"* he said, glancing over the ash pile of his shoulder at the blaze. A single tear left a trail down his grimy cheek. Without warning he lurched toward David with outstretched arms, *"Tenez,* take it. I'm going back."

The Englishman's hands encircled the velvet plush. He looked down and saw the Star of David appliqued in gilt thread, less two of its points—burnt away.

"Don't let it fall," ordered the asbestos gnome and was gone.

There was no question of abandoning his charge. He carried the bundle through the smoke, which grew denser, choking. A crowd had gathered on the street, gray figures feeling their way through an unnatural twilight, figures without faces, murmuring, crying out. He felt no pain. The sirens blared louder, louder… Holding fast he smothered what remained of the embers. The swaddled scrolls, seared but intact, rested against his chest like a sleeping child.

An elderly couple pressed through the crowd, speaking in rapid French. David recognized the word *Torah*.

"Je vais prendre ça," said the old man, stepping forward with a low wheeze.

David nestled his cheek against the wounded star and felt his composure ebb.

"Did you not hear me? I will take that."

The correct response would have been to relinquish the scrolls, but instead David tightened his grip.

The man's wife peered up at him through red-rimmed eyes. "It's all right, we're members of the congregation. We will see that they're safe."

"Of course," David conceded.

No sooner had he let go the Torah than his hands began to smart. Spurred by the pain he wove through the crowd, wanting only to fill his lungs and flee. A trio of fire engines screeched to a halt nearby. Already the police were erecting barricades. At the end of the street he took a last look at *Bet Shalom*, its windows shattered, soot blackening its stones, and felt a slow tremor descend the gradient of his spine. He turned the corner. A side of pork hung collecting flies in the window of the neighborhood *boucherie*.

He found the estate car where he had left it. Its windscreen, rent down the middle in an angry zigzag, held no reflection. He slipped inside, locked the door, and examined his face in the rearview mirror. He looked into his own eyes, into the blue-gray depths of his unlidded soul, and whispered, "Fraud."

◆

The house in France David could have bought years ago, but the lover was slow to reveal herself, seemed always elsewhere. He set out in search of her with nothing but the sketchiest of criteria: that she be touchable, laughter-prone, that she read books. He prowled the libraries. London's tendered all the melancholy of a Russian novel. Winter blew in and on impulse he booked a British Airways flight to Miami, thawed for a few days, then slowly, with no fixed itinerary, made his way north. By Boxing Day he had reached New England.

He liked the austere little villages, the serious-looking people with their stout shoes and raingear; he liked that he was not in England yet oddly "at home." He found the women refreshingly unfashionable, which made them easier to approach. They responded to his accent, didn't hesitate to ask questions—no one could fault their friendliness—but after a cup of coffee or two, it would surface that one was engaged, another in therapy... what was the point in taking it further?

He was nearing the Canadian border and about to reverse direction when he caught sight of a small whitewashed library, a forlorn little box of a place with nothing but a weathercock to adorn it. More from habit than hope he parked his rental car and stepped inside. A youngish blonde woman at the information desk looked up from a stack of reference books but didn't deign to acknowledge him. The first thing he noticed about her was the caressing, almost carnal, way her hands turned the pages. There was nothing untoward about her makeup or dress; her appearance, in fact, was rather prim, which only made her corporeal subtext the more maddening. He walked past her and pretended to browse the stacks until the lights dimmed and a gray-haired librarian in Birkenstocks and leg warmers gently put him out. He went back the next day. On the third day, having confirmed his impression of the previous two, he composed himself, walked up to the counter where the blonde stood sorting index cards, and said, "I'm looking for a book."

He had expected his foreignness to elicit the usual curiosity, but her only response was, "Title?"

He didn't know the title.

"Author?"

He didn't know that either.

She had remained businesslike. "Subject?"

"I'm not sure what you'd call it, a book for people who never quite get it right—how to up-end your life? Conscious turmoil?"

"Can't help you," she said and resumed her sorting. "How-to books aren't my area."

David began to walk away, but in his fantasies she had already laid him open like a time-stiffened tome. Though she might feign indifference, they were part of the same story. "What *is* your area?"

"Officially, historical fiction." She lowered her voice to a whisper. "But I've been told I'm not a bad kisser."

He had found her, and her name was Rowena. She was thirty years old, overripe and nobody's heroine. He courted her, and slowly, not without resistance, she opened to him like a late-blooming orchid. That the rest would be easy, a mere matter of logistics, he never doubted.

◆

The Volvo lurched onto the highway with David at the wheel, knowing neither where he was going nor which side of the white line would take him there. Traffic thinned to a trickle. A blanket of smog had formed above the skyline. He drove with a dull ache behind his eyes.

Only marginally aware of his surroundings, he passed a *hypermarché*, a home improvement store, a petrol station...

he might have been anywhere. Soon all Europe would look like this, smell like this; men in windbreakers would lurk in every alley waiting to set one ablaze. He had to speak to someone, put a stop to it. He found himself in a police station, at a loss to say how he had arrived. There was a staleness about the place, as of cigarette butts and desiccated rodents. Reams of yellowing paper spilled from drawers. A man in a flat-topped hat sat opposite him, filling in forms.

"These bruises on your face?" The copper glanced at him for an instant, but David couldn't see his expression, only a broad black hat brim ending in Dumbo ears.

"Two men assaulted me—the same men who firebombed the synagogue."

"Shall I call a doctor?"

"No. I'm fine. A little shaken, that's all."

Flat-top stopped writing and murmured to a colleague at the next desk, "A witness." Turning back to David, "Then you can identify them?"

David strained to picture his assailants' faces but saw only the glint of metal, the dreary crisscrossing of chain links.

"Surely you remember *something?*"

"Their eyes."

"What about their eyes?"

"They might have been razor wire."

"Ah, Arabs." The policemen exchanged a knowing look.

David's mind refused to make the connection; after all, weren't Arabs also Semites? He thought of his former assistant, Hassan, of his physician, Dr. Mahmoud, such cultivated people, hardly the sort to go hurling homemade bombs. "I never said they were Arabs," he protested. "They spoke French."

"*Quelque chose de plus?*"

"I'd seen one of them earlier, near the salvage yard."

"*Ah*, an Arab neighborhood."

"Surely one can't draw conclusions based on that alone."

"This is hardly an isolated incident, *monsieur*. The streets of France have become a second Jerusalem." Lowering his head over the forms, Flat-top ticked off a row of boxes. "Sign here."

"They said terrible things—don't you want to know?"

"If you wish to add comments." His square thumb flattened against a dotted line.

David scrawled a few tired phrases, signed the report, and handed it back. "What happens now?"

"We have your details." The form vanished into a manila folder labeled 05/17/2000.

"I see, but what next?"

The policeman, cracking his knuckles in rapid succession, ran his shadowy gaze along David's bruises. "Are you sure you would not like a doctor, *monsieur?*"

David walked out into a late-afternoon downpour. He got into his car, locked the door, and mopped his face and neck. By the time he pulled back onto the highway, the rain had stopped. Threads of steam rose from the asphalt.

The way home was all strangeness, a protracted blind turn. Through his cracked windscreen he watched the city disperse, and the sky swell to bursting. The road narrowed. Up ahead, he could see crosses so tall they pierced the clouds. *Vis a tergo,* the monks whispered from their wrappings. *Vis a tergo...* The green hills parted as if a fault line had opened at their center; the margins caved in. Anchoring himself to a dim sliver of moon, he cut the engine and coasted.

LIONEL STAYS LATE AT THE RIVER

Beautemps' quartet of wrought-iron streetlamps came

on, revealing a legion of dragonflies dancing in spirals. The sky deepened from sapphire to ebony as the North Star broke through. Somewhere a jazz ballad whined, adding brass to the river's rhythmic cackle.

When Lionel was not serving the *intérêt general* as mayor of his village, he could be found at the river, eking out a livelihood by renting canoes. Having beached his boats for the day, he transferred the contents of the cash box—68 euro, two business cards, and a scribbled IOU—to his pocket. Hardly a windfall, but not bad for so early in the season. The siege would begin soon enough. In the space of fifteen years he had grown his fleet from two to an even dozen, each vessel christened with the name of a place he had known: Wallis, Bora-Bora, Adelie Land, Mayotte... His office, no more than a shack, smelled faintly of algae. He had painted the walls an aqueous blue-green; on the north side a stuffed barracuda stared down with a fixed expression. His wife Laura had been after him for years to throw the creature out, but homesick for the open sea, he would sooner have parted with his own teeth. Returning the box to its place beneath the counter, he gave the fish a perfunctory salute.

"All present and correct, *mon brave.*"

He switched off the one bare bulb, stepped out, and padlocked the door behind him.

The evening was mild, the air held hints of rain and wild rosemary. Purple shadows spilled down the walls of the gorge. He began to ascend the step-path, a makeshift affair that seemed always on the verge of collapse. Twice last season he had dedicated a day to replacing the railroad ties and tamping down the earth, but then that caravan of gypsies had come through, seven children to each adult and the whole lot clambering up and down like mandrills. Midway, he stumbled and his eye lit on a figure in silhouette: a man seated on a ledge with legs dangling into the abyss.

"*Attention!* " the Frenchman called out. "I wouldn't trust that rock if I were you."

"Good evening, Lionel," a voice drifted back. The man climbed down from the ledge and began to walk in his direction.

Lionel strained in the low light to make out his features. *"C'est toi*, David?"

"I'm afraid so."

The response struck the Frenchman as odd but not unduly so. That the English have a humor all their own, he knew from long experience. "Stargazing, my friend?"

"Dawdling."

At the top of the path they converged, and David extended a hand. The grip, Lionel couldn't help but notice, lacked its usual gusto. "Are you all right? Your face... have you had an accident?"

"Is it bad?" David took a handkerchief from his pocket and began to daub randomly at his jaw and cheeks. "I wouldn't want to give Rowena and mother a fright."

"Come home with me." Lionel took him firmly by the arm. "Laura and I will fix you up." They continued their ascent in tandem. In the dim light it was hard to assess the extent of David's injuries. As they reached the main road, the Englishman lifted a hand to shield his eyes from the streetlamp's wan beam. Concussion, Lionel thought, possible shock.

"Awfully good of you," David murmured.

"Did you leave your car nearby?" Lionel pivoted, searching for the familiar green tank.

"I don't know—can't remember."

"But you have the keys." David seemed surprised to find them in his hand. "You were in the city earlier, *non*? I saw you head south."

"Yes, the city..."

To Lionel's relief, he spotted the Volvo beside the war memorial. "I'll drive." As they approached the car he glanced again at David. "That's quite a nasty crack in your windscreen—it was an auto accident you had?"

"Not exactly."

"*C'est pas grave*, I have a friend who replaces glass. I'll phone in the morning."

The drive to *Rue Moulin à Huile*, where Lionel lived with his wife in the converted olive oil mill, could not have been more than a few hundred meters away, but cowed by the car's right-hand drive he doubled back and entered from the far side where the road was widest. As he parked he felt the injured man's fingertips graze his shirtsleeve.

"Tell me, Lionel, do you consider me somehow, fundamentally, different from yourself?"

Thinking he had misheard, he cut the engine. "*Pardon?*" The Englishman, stumbling over the syllables, repeated the question. "David, David..." Lionel hedged, "you're English—not as English as the others, *bien sûr.*"

"Meaning?"

"You mix."

"Would you pick me out on the street, at a glance?"

He studied David's face, straining to detect in it the least abnormality. "Not likely, but why do you ask? What has happened?"

"Another time, Lionel," David said in a tone of apology. "I'm not up to talking right now. If Laura asks, let's just say an accident—at the river, perhaps."

"As you like, *mon ami*. But next time you need something, tell me. Leclerc from the council goes to the city on business all the time."

Relieved to be home, Lionel stepped from the Volvo onto the cobblestone lane. David followed, not quite steady on his feet. At the curb Lionel took his friend by the shoulders and examined the subtly rearranged proportions of his face. "Whatever it was, you're fine. It's over. Forget it."

They turned up the front path, treading their own shadows. Thank you, Lionel," said the Englishman. "Thank you very much indeed."

But was it over? Barely had they reached the privet when Laura opened the door, her thick chestnut hair upswept and the nape so vulnerable Lionel could not help but cradle it.

"My latest casualty," he said with forced levity, nudging David forward.

Taking the injured man in tow, Laura examined his face from forehead to chin. "*Mon pauvre*, but what happened?"

"A boating mishap," Lionel hastened to say. "I should refuse to rent to the English. Every season some *imbécile* comes to the river from Leeds or London and drowns in three feet of water. They do not float these descendants of Nelson; one would think they are punctured."

"Punctured," parroted David.

"But you're entirely dry," Laura observed. "And your hand—isn't that a burn?"

Lionel respected his wife too much to deceive her, but for David's sake he maintained the ruse. "David didn't actually capsize. You know how the rocks jut out on the north side, and that current…"

"Of course," she rejoined, "the rocks, the current."

David looked from one to the other, his gaze vaguely unfocused. "If you could just clean me up a bit."

Laura, taking charge, tugged the patient gently toward an armchair. "Sit, David." Then to her husband, "A glass of brandy, *Capitaine*. I'll get the rest." She excused herself and returned moments later with a bottle of rubbing alcohol, another of iodine, a tube of ointment, and a skein of absorbent cotton. "This may sting," she warned. "Drink up."

The doctoring took no more than a few minutes. David, stoic by birth, sedated by the liquor, submitted without a wince, waxed oddly cheerful. "I'm fit as a fetter," he declared, getting to his feet. "Or do I mean fiddle?"

"No need to rush off," said Laura.

"Truly, I'm fine."

Lionel loaned him a clean shirt and walked him out, noting with concern his starboard tilt and off-course gait. "Let me drive you home," he hastened to say, but David wouldn't hear of it.

"I'm fine, truly. Fit as a—"

"I know, I know. Chess tomorrow?"

"Usual time."

Lionel waited on the curb while David arranged himself behind the steering wheel. The tank pulled slowly away, negotiating the corner only after several reverses. The bells chimed nine and nine again. Charged with a sudden urgency, he turned and raced back toward the house. Laura would be warming over his dinner, setting a place for him, lighting a candle. There were stars in the birdbath, shards of moon on the doorstep. Moist-eyed without alibi he threw open the door, hung his cap on a hook, and kicked off his deck shoes.

His wife, framed in the kitchen entryway like a monument to forbearance, crossed her supple arms. "Now tell me, what *really* happened to David Crown?"

ROWENA HEARS CONFESSION

An unfamiliar bouquet of ripening fruit and river water wafted through the shutters. Rowena parted the gauze curtain and looked out. The gnarled trees stood silhouetted against an undefined beyond—alive, pulsing, black. Into that teasing unknown, silent but for the *churr* of cicadas, David had vanished. She hadn't seen him since morning, had barely thought of him, but suddenly, piqued by the bright splinter moon, she wondered if he was lost, hungry, or if the night had worked its voodoo and carried him away. She had read about men going off like that, deciding in the space of a breath to abandon wife, children, livelihood… a hankering takes them and their lives implode. Years later they turn up repentant on a doorstep—but that was in books.

There was no one in the house but David's mother Miriam, only empty rooms and the ghosts that drifted through them like dust. She had never lived in a place so old, so rambling. Not even her dreams could fill it. How keyed-up David had seemed that morning, and where was it he said he was going? If Rowena didn't remember, how much less likely that Miriam would.

Pulling on a cotton kimono she crossed the crewel rug, opened the bedroom door, and gazed down the corridor. Shadows. She stepped out, palpating the wall as far as the staircase. As her eyes adjusted she saw a mouse scrabble down the far wall and disappear behind a hung tapestry. She was about to retrace her steps when the front door opened and David stepped soundlessly inside. Slender in profile, he bent at the waist to remove his shoes.

"Why so late?"

Startled, he glanced about. "Complications." Then lowering his voice, "Mother asleep?"

He ascended the stairs weaving between the handrails, took her by the shoulder, and pulled gently toward the bedroom, closing the door behind them. She reached for a light switch.

"No," he said sharply.

"No light? Fine." Mistaking his agitation for ardor, she began to undress.

"Later perhaps." His voice, though softer, seemed not

his at all.

Her discarded robe lay in a tangle at her feet, the fly of her denim shorts flapped open. Stepping clear, she flicked on a lamp.

David veered and padded to the window.

She rifled the dresser drawer for a nightdress. "What kept you?"

He stood with his back to her, hunched over the sill. "I'm a fraud, Rowena, not of my own making but complicit. My father's great grandfather was a rabbi. I had relatives in Poland, in Hungary, who died in the Holocaust. I even had a bar mitzvah of sorts—my mother arranged it on the sly. My father never knew."

"Why bring it up now? Religion has never been an issue."

"Cohen, my father was a Cohen. Crown came later, once he'd started making money. When we moved to Henley, my mother stopped lighting candles on the Sabbath. My father would scold her if she used a Yiddish expression, an endearment. Who were we fooling? People *knew*."

Rowena didn't like where the discussion was going. They had found common ground in humanism, and she saw no reason to dwell on their differences. "Look at me." He half turned, not quite meeting her eyes. "What does it matter? I was Catholic once. A person grows beyond any stock set of beliefs."

"Yes—no. I *am* a Jew. It's not a suit of clothes I can put on and take off. Maybe Christians can, but I'm not allowed that indulgence."

"You're shaking."

"What must a person sacrifice to fit in? Who is David Crown? Neither an Englishman nor a Jew. An invention— but whose?"

"Look at me, will you?" He faced her with an

expression pitiful and defiant in equal parts. "Jesus." She stepped closer, cupped his chin in both hands as if to trap it. "Jesus, what happened to you?"

He lowered his head. "I'm so tired, Rowena."

She leaned her cheek against his shoulder and felt a hollow open to nestle her. "It's late. We'll talk tomorrow."

He seemed grateful for the reprieve, though he said nothing more. In bed his body sought hers if only to spoon. His skin sweated cold. Torn limbless from a dream, she jarred awake. A wayward gust of wind had overturned the antique washstand; the pitcher had lost its spout; water pooled in the crevices of the stone floor. Beside her, David curled like a fetus, his voice muted by sleep. She lowered an ear to his mouth and felt his breath caress the lobe. She listened deeply. From where do they come, these plagiarized messages rife with meaning and menace? A tremor passed over David's lips. His words found a rhythm and echoed like a mantra: "*Vis a tergo, vis a tergo…*" She had read the mystics, knew how easily a person might switch realms, rational one day, sleeping on nettles the next.

Still murmuring he rolled over. She rounded the bed, crouched down, and studied his bruised and sleep-swollen face: ordinary, the features symmetrical, the nose prominent—but only slightly. A Jewish face? Descended from a rabbi, he had said.

"*Vis a tergo, vis a tergo…*"

She shook him awake.

"Don't!" he cried, raising his hands like a shield.

"It's okay." She took the hands to her bosom, held them there while the tension drained away. "You were talking in your sleep. Where did you learn Latin?"

"Harrow. It was my worst subject."

"One line must have stuck."

He pulled himself up and his bare chest emerged from

the duvet. His back thudded against the headboard. "I suppose I owe you an explanation—but what does it mean?"

"A force from behind."

The paler of his cheeks flashed red.

"Are you all right?" Willing to be put off no longer, Rowena took him by the shoulders. "What the heck happened to you?"

He recounted the events of the previous day. The assault, from what she gathered, lasted no more than a few minutes. The synagogue fared worse. David had lain unconscious nearby, driven to a police station, filled in some papers, and it was over. She suspected he had spared her some unsavory detail, a profanity, some petty humiliation, but she didn't press for more. What he described was not the France she knew, village France with its painted shutters, tidy streets, and placid routines.

"But that's the city," she hastened to say. "Nothing like that could happen in Beautemps."

David looked unsure.

"You're home now. Home and safe."

"It's an illusion, safety." There was something in his voice she had never heard before—obduracy, cynicism? A hardness, in any case.

"People can be all sorts and still get along," she felt obliged to remind him. "Most do."

"There's no telling what will provoke a confrontation: the bridge of one's nose, a posture, an accent…"

"Stop talking like that. Nothing has changed; it's the same world out there. You liked it well enough yesterday." She pulled on a robe, sashed it, and started for the door. "I'll just put some ice on that bump."

"Not now. We'll be late getting to breakfast."

"But your face—"

"We'll tell my mother that I skidded into a cross, one

of those crosses as you leave the village. I skidded, and a tree branch swiped the windscreen. That will do. We had a sun shower yesterday, didn't we? The roads will have had to be slick." Satisfied, he got up and stepped into his leather slippers.

She squared off with him. "No, David."

"It's a plausible story."

"Stop it, I won't be your accomplice in this fabrication. Your mother is sufficiently batty without your compounding her fantasies. And you—the sooner you accept what's happened, the sooner you can get on with your life."

"You don't understand."

"What happened to you could have happened to anyone," she insisted. "Why take it so personally?"

He lowered his head and rubbed the furrow from his brow. He pushed back his thinning fringe of hair. There was something unsettling about his containment. To touch him then would have been like uncorking a bottle of warm champagne.

"Shall I bring your coffee?"

He trudged slowly toward her, a look of umbrage lending shadow to his bruised face. Only a pool of sunlight separated them. Gazing past her, he sidestepped and continued forward. She heard the tap creak on. "Won't be a minute," his voice drifted back.

DAVID'S MORNING AFTER

What happens to a man whose very identity is violated? What happens once he picks himself up and hobbles off, appearing on the surface barely changed, and yet inside a vacancy? Is he now a Jew because someone spat the term at him? And if he is not a Jew, what then?

On the accustomed day the bread truck rumbled by, its

radio blasting American rock, and the tempting aromas of butter and walnuts trailing in its wake. All along the cobbled lanes old women laid aside their embroidery hoops and remote controls, hooked a net shopping sack onto their wrists, and emerged from their front doors with grim determination, sights set on the crustiest baguettes, the flakiest croissants. Watching them, David thought of raptors. Once, transfixed by a *National Geographic* video, he had seen buzzards peck the last morsel of flesh from a fox's carcass.

He waited for the truck to continue its rounds, then needing to walk, slipped unseen from the house. It was nearly noon; already the villagers had begun to disappear behind their latched shutters. Dogs prowled the gutters for left-behind crumbs.

Vaguely affronted by the rows of closed shutters, by the scavenging dogs with their busy wet noses, he steered toward the village's wooded outskirts and the solitude they afforded.

"Mr. Crown!" Hedy's inimitable alto. Bent on encounter, she intercepted him to the north of the war memorial. At close range she was all cleavage and breath, a veritable storm surge of pheromones. "Missed the bread truck?"

"Just getting some fresh air."

"I have something for you." With a myopic squint she nudged aside a pair of baguettes and rifled through her tote bag. "I've been thinking about your foyer..." She thrust a trio of paint swatches into his hands. "The walls are a bit off, don't you think? It's so important that the palette be right, suggestive of the period, yet at the same time *à la page.*"

He fingered the swatches absently.

"No hasty decisions," she said. "I wouldn't want to impose my taste, but they're perfect, so *Vie Dorée.*"

How to escape without eliciting a further onslaught of beneficence? He wanted nothing more than distance—from

Hedy, from the demands of social intercourse. He readied his stock of polite evasions, but a sudden distraction spared him. Blurred by the speed of his flight, Russ Griffith streamed by in his signature running gear en route to the charcuterie. Taking David by an elbow, Hedy tugged toward the shadows, into the cool green mouth of a small park. "Let's hibernate for a moment, shall we?"

"I really shouldn't—"

"Has he borrowed money from you yet?"

"Who, Russ?"

"He has, hasn't he? I should have warned you sooner. Don't expect to get a penny back."

David shrugged, one of those noncommittal half gestures.

"Horses," she went on. "Our American friend's got it bad for the horses. Poor Deirdre's been bled dry—it's her money, you know—and the rest of us… well, one learns to avoid him after a time."

"I really must be getting on." To make his point he began to walk away.

She clung to him like a bead of rain on an umbrella. "Why don't I join you? No use your skulking around solo."

"Some other time. I was just about to head home."

"Bit turned around, aren't you? Look, I heard what happened to you in the city—your mother must be beside herself. A pretty sight you're not. If you ask me, the Arabs are out of control in this country."

"Arabs? I don't know for a fact they were Arabs."

"Well, I heard they were Arabs." She was beginning to sound irritated, though she chose that moment to unfurl an ear-to-ear smile. "Anyway, use common sense: Can you see the French flinging themselves on people like that? It doesn't happen."

"*Anything* can and does happen."

Still smiling, she clucked her tongue. "My but we're surly today."

"Why is everyone so eager to pass this off as a spat between Arabs and Jews? How convenient to blame one minority for the misfortunes of another."

"Who do *you* blame?"

"It's not a question of blame but truth." His voice cracked, its pittance of ire spent. He ran a hand across his lips as if to seal them. "You're right, I *am* surly today. Forgive me. Please convey my regards to Cecil."

Stranded on a blade of grass, David waited for a bell to toll or a stray dog to nip his heel. He felt the weight of his own shadow. The precise verticality of Hedy's stance, the molten glint in her eyes, told him he would not be forgiven.

When he arrived home, his mother was prowling the corridors in a white nylon slip and wellies. Spotting him, her brow bunched like old upholstery. "They wouldn't come here, would they?"

He knew whom she meant by "they"—Nazis in all their various guises past and present, the many-faced bogeyman even a Holocaust could not sate. "Of course not," he hastened to assure her.

"But they could."

"Madame Fermat is a fortress. No one gets by her."

She seemed to mull this.

"Come, I'll walk you to your room and you can get dressed."

Her withered arms rose on reflex to crisscross her bosom. "I can find my own room," she said, her tone wavering between apology and rebuke. "Tea at four. English time."

A Monument to Solitude

David Crown was often on Lionel's mind those bright, waxing days heralding summer. He hadn't come by for their scheduled game of chess, nor had he called to excuse himself. His home lay between the *mairie* and the river; Lionel would pass it again and again in the course of manning his two posts. From a distance it appeared a citadel, remnant of some fabled golden city. In full sunlight it gleamed. Only up close could one appreciate its essential simplicity. David had not tampered with the façade; it wore none of the reproduction frippery favored by the other English. But had he brought the chateau "alive?" Were it not for David's lugubrious green tank parked in the driveway, it might have been a monument to solitude.

Lionel was not expected back until two p.m. at the *mairie*, where for the remainder of the afternoon he would sit behind a mahogany desk to dredge his way through correspondence. The job of mayor was not so much onerous as wearying, always the same petty feuds, the same jockeying for advantage. After a decade, a disgruntled neighbor whom he once fined for hunting out of season still pissed against his outside wall.

It was not Lionel's custom to drop by unannounced, but he had an hour to spare and would have liked nothing more than to spend it with David, talking soccer or current events. Surely the company would do them both good. Removing his cap, he stepped up to the massive oak door and knocked.

A voice, rough and unthrottled, called out, *"Attendez!"* A command, make no mistake. The door jarred open. Grasping the knob with a dust cloth, Madame Fermat pulled herself up with inflated dignity.

He greeted her formally, as he might the wife of a

notable, though the housekeeper's husband never amounted to more than a glorified houseboy, grooming the hunting dogs of a local wine baron. Madame Fermat herself, a virtual foreigner, having emigrated from the Alsace during the war, could claim no distinction other than an overly long widowhood. Destined to spend her old age tending other women's houses, she had drawn about her person an iron self-importance.

"And Mr. Crown?" he asked, still planted on the doorstep.

"Resting, one supposes."

He glanced past her into the spacious foyer, which renovated to perfection smelled of lemon oil and fresh roses.

"The whole family *comme des morts*." The housekeeper gestured toward the staircase with a backhanded swipe of her cloth. "I've never worked for English. This is how they are, *non?*"

"*C'est normal* at this hour."

The housekeeper rested a fist on each of her side-of-beef hips. "At all hours."

"Must be the heat; they're not accustomed to it. Give them time."

"It has gotten worse these past days," she said, muffling her indiscretion with a cupped hand. "The *monsieur* beaten about the face... a brawl, one supposes."

He silenced her with a raised index finger. "Nothing of the sort." Concerned for David, he had called friends in the city and made inquiries. "*Beurs*, Arabs. An assault."

"*C'est pas vrai!*"

"It's out of hand: Toulouse, Marseilles, Montpellier..."

"But why the *monsieur?*"

He thought it best to skirt the particulars. "A social problem, no reflection on David Crown."

"A woman needs to feel that she is working in a respectable home."

"I entirely understand."

The housekeeper nodded stiffly, extracted her spray bottle, and began to polish the door's brass fittings.

Over her shoulder he watched David weave distractedly down the marble staircase. "Did I hear someone at the door?"

Madame Fermat stepped reluctantly aside. "*Monsieur le Maire* to see you."

"Come in, Lionel. What can I offer you? Too early for a pastis, how about—?

"Nothing. I was on my way home."

"You must be hungry. How about—?"

"I can't stay. Have you heard anything from the police?"

David's brow faintly lifted.

"It's a small village, my friend. News travels. You're not the first victim. Every time the Israelis crack down on the Palestinians, some kid from the projects gets it into his head to assault a Jew or to desecrate a Jewish grave. The streets of France have become a second Jerusalem."

"That's what the police said.

"They would know, *n'est-ce pas?* The *flics* can't even get into the bad Arab neighborhoods; they're impenetrable as fiefdoms."

David's back stiffened. "I'm still not convinced—no matter, let's not go into it."

"Stick to the French areas," Lionel told him, "and you should have no trouble."

"There's something I've been wanting to ask you." David knit and unknit his discordant fingers. "A favor."

Always a giver, David had never before made a single request.

"I've been thinking about those boys at the synagogue."

"I suppose you heard about the confession?"

He hadn't.

"The police were right—and wrong. The bomber who confessed was a mixed race boy, seventeen years old, father Algerian, mother French."

"And the accomplice?"

"His younger brother, not yet sixteen. Fell in with a gang and got his face carved up—that's what prompted the elder's confession. He didn't know how else to get the kid off the streets."

"A noble impulse."

"Noble and futile. Minors get half the adult sentence, if any, under *l'excuse de minorité*. For a first offence they could be out in a matter of weeks." It seemed best to change the subject, but David wasn't about to let it drop.

"Can I visit them?"

Lionel's first impulse was to protect David, to spare him the unblunted anger of two penned-up adolescents nursing a gripe against the world. "What good would it do? It's up to the authorities now."

The Englishman gazed into his open palms. "It's up to all of us."

"David, David... this is bigger than you. You don't know these people, their *mentalité*, their *histoire*. We give them jobs, we give them rights, and this is how they repay us."

"I don't know about the others, but these two—they're just kids. Can you arrange a meeting? Please."

"Let me see what I can do." Lionel knew even then he was inviting disaster, but David was a friend, and a pig-headed one at that. He would learn the hard way that not every living soul was redeemable. He would learn and pay the price.

Madame Fermat, her hands gloved in kitchen mitts,

strode back into the foyer. "Monsieur's luncheon is getting cold."

Lionel wished them both good day and set off down the driveway. At the gate he paused and could not resist a backward glance. In the scorching light the *Vie Dorée* cast a shadow so long it skirted the war memorial. As he watched, its shutters closed one by one.

THE PRICE OF TRUFFLES

It was the wrong time for a party, but the invitation had lain on the kitchen table for three weeks. Hedy and Cecil Rhodes, the first English couple to acquire a home in Beautemps' old quarter, entertained only once each season. To decline at short notice would have relegated a newcomer to the social fringe for years.

David put on a stoic face, bought flowers and champagne for the hosts, and held out his arm to Rowena. "You shall be the toast of the village, my rose."

Doubting, she took David's arm and said nothing.

Maison Joyeuse had the calculated provincial chic showcased on magazine covers. Cecil Rhodes, posed poolside like an updated Gatsby, took David's champagne and avidly studied its label. "Decent of you, old boy, but don't you find Bollinger a tad overrated?"

The party bound together for the space of several interminable hours a mismatched assortment of part-time residents, who under other circumstances might gladly have avoided one another. A succession of well-heeled Europeans introduced themselves, all with the same air of birthright and amour-propre. Somewhere on the fringe loitered a token American jock, whose sole contribution of the evening was to monopolize the hors d'oeuvres tray, denuding it of smoked oysters.

Dinner was a sit-down affair with place cards. Rowena found herself separated from David with Hedy driven between them like a wedge. On her opposite side sat the Dutch farmer, whose patched blue jeans and bowl haircut made him an object of stares and whispers. His name, overlong with a dearth of vowels, boggled the tongue. For more than a decade he had been planting oak and hazelnut trees inoculated with mycelium spore, hoping for that rare symbiosis, fungus filament, that produces truffles.

La Rhodes swiveled in her seat to say, "So, Swijdendorp, when can we expect the celebratory banquet? I'm quite fond of truffles, you know."

"Hard to predict," the farmer replied softly.

From the far side of the table Cecil took up the thread. "But it's been ages, old boy."

"There's no set timetable. I can to a point create the conditions—plant the trees, tend the undergrowth—but there is still an element of mystery."

"Ages it's been. All that sniffing around for spores…"

As their host erupted in laughter, his wife, her mouth otherwise occupied, faintly rolled her eyes. The Dutchman hunched over his plate. "I have dogs for that."

"Mutts, aren't they?"

"Any dog with good search abilities and a brisk stride can be trained."

"But waiting ten years for a first harvest," David ruminated aloud, "and the risk involved. Few people would have your fortitude."

The farmer shrugged. "Until the truffles take hold, I grow a little sorghum, a little wheat, enough to get by."

Hedy had taken a lingering sip of Burgundy. "With truffle prices what they are—1200 euros per kilo, last I checked—Swijdendorp will buy us all out one day. But can't we speak of something else? All this talk of fungus…"

"Hardly an appetite stimulant," parleyed her husband.

"And I have the most glorious peach flan in the Aga."

Over dessert *La Rhodes* turned her attention to Rowena. "David tells me you write. He was rather vague about what it is you're working on, something to do with the French revolution?"

"A novel based on the life of Charlotte Corday."

"Didn't she kill someone?"

"Marat. *L'Ami du Peuple.*"

"That's right. In his bath, wasn't it?" Bosom first, she swiveled toward David. "Are you fond of long soaks in the tub, Mr. Crown?"

Laughter rippled up and down the table. The oyster thief whispered to his wife, a platinum blonde in Spandex, and the pair, openly drunk and not caring who noticed, woozily knocked heads.

Licking custard from his lips, Cecil waggled a fork in Rowena's direction. "Why Corday? Surely there were more prominent figures in the revolution and longer-lived ones. Corday interests me about as much as yesterday's suicide bomber, but then, martyrs have always depressed me."

She could feel Swijdendorp's eyes probe the nape of her neck. He had pushed back his chair, revealing both frayed knees of his unfashionable jeans. "According to medical journals," she soldiered on, "depression is the result of suppressed anger, hardly an indicator of literary merit." The tines of Cecil's fork pinged against his water glass. "The ready availability of Prozac makes grist of even the most maudlin subject."

There was no comeback, not a murmur. David, carefully refolding his dinner napkin, turned to *La Rhodes* with the requisite smile. "I'm afraid we must be going. Madame Fermat gets off at ten. Thank you for having us— please stay seated, we'll show ourselves out."

The hostess clasped David by a lapel and kissed him thrice, alternating cheeks. "Watch yourself, Mr. Crown, your Arabs have struck again. It was in the paper." To Rowena she drawled, "Charmed, darling."

Swijdendorp shadowed them to the door, where he donned a lopsided canvas hat.

"I'd like to see your outfit sometime," David said to him. "Get behind the mystique to the nuts and bolts."

The Dutchman only yawned. "Fences to mend to-morrow," he remarked absently, walking past them into a moonless night.

LIONEL KEEPS WATCH

Laura, after teaching Social Studies for twenty years, took a research job for an author of some renown, a *soizante-huitard* who had yet to shed his ponytail. Not someone Lionel admired. But he could no more impose a vocation on his wife than he could dictate her politics. Each morning she set to work over stacks of journals and manuscript pages, wielding her yellow highlighting marker with a pugilist's aplomb. Afternoons she spent combing the university libraries for obscure libels. Seldom did she return home until late evening. Of necessity Lionel resurrected his meager culinary skills, learned on kitchen detail during a turbulent stint in the Indian Ocean.

The sky dimmed, unperturbed by the half moon that had risen only to spill across the rooftops like hollandaise. Laura swept through the door with a baguette tucked beneath an arm and tendrils of hair streaming free from her pinned chignon. He watched her from his vantage point at the kitchen stove, a voyeur in his own home riveted by the unassuming sensuality of his own wife.

"*Ça va, Capitaine?*" Her lips grazed his cheek.

"That slave-driver keep you late again?"

She rubbed past him, opened the refrigerator door, and rifled the crisper for salad fixings. "I make my own hours."

Coming up behind her, he unpinned her hair and let it flow silken into his open palms. "Your boss, Foussier, is an old hell raiser. His books infuriate people; he intends them to."

She removed her treasure from his hands, filled them instead with jars of oil and vinegar. "Prepare the dressing?"

"It's a new millennium. You would think he'd trim his beard, at least."

"Shall we open the Burgundy?"

"And that paunch of his…"

Laura lit tapers, and they sat down at the dining room table. Lionel picked at whatever was on his plate. A passing car bombarded them with rap music. The table sprawled barren to the oasis of his wife's lips. He watched the fork move in and out of her mouth amid flashes of tongue. "Long week?" she asked.

"Like any other. You? I've never seen you so engrossed in your work, or is it Foussier you're taken with?"

She set down her cutlery. "Have I been neglecting you, *Capitaine*?"

"*Non, Matelot.*"

"*Alors?*"

"I'm a practical man. Extremists unsettle my nerves. Life is a balancing act; why set it topsy-turvy with far-fetched ideas?"

"Your dinner is getting cold."

"What is it about Foussier's work that draws you so?"

"The shades of gray," she said without hesitation. "Think back to how we were taught history… the Second World War: The resistance fighters were heroes, the collaborators family men at worst. And Vichy? Vichy was a last-ditch effort to avert bloodshed and destruction, a political necessity. But *Maréchal* Petain was so old, a puppet in the hands of the Gestapo—which leaves the French blameless. True?"

"Something like that."

"Pap."

"These are our grandparents you're talking about!"

"*Exactement.*" She inclined toward him looking calm and factual, like the schoolteacher she had once been. "Foussier has collected personal accounts, thousands of them, from people very much like our grandparents."

"What's the point now? There will be no more wars in Europe, not with the EU."

"Foussier says until we accept our past, the present can't be more than an echo. How else to explain the current of fascism rippling across the *new* Europe?"

"France has never been fascist!"

"*Calme-toi,* Lionel."

"Foussier can get stuffed. We French grant the same rights to everyone without exception. We keep a close eye on Le Pen and his ilk, on the handful of skinheads who have yet to outgrow their dogmatism. Never could there be a French Hitler. We are not Germans, asking to be led by the nose to perdition. Life is stubborn in us. We go our own way."

"Then how do you explain French ultra-nationalism?"

"People letting off steam."

"How do you explain David Crown's bloodied face?"

He set down his wine glass, and a spill of Burgundy bled into the pale tablecloth. Laura pushed back her chair and walked to the kitchen, returning moments later with a moistened dishcloth.

"Here, let me help," he said.

They cleared the table in silence, letting the argument rest. Laura sectioned an apple, cut a wedge of Camembert.

He switched on the radio to *France Bleue*.

"How *is* David?" she asked.

"Better. Fit as a fettuccine."

They converged on the sofa, his hand gravitating to the camber of her thigh, her cheek nesting in the crook of his shoulder. Laura murmured, "I don't like to think of him poking around that prison... the harshness of things."

"It has all been arranged. My friends will keep an eye on him."

"How would David feel if he knew he was being spied on?"

Lionel touched a finger to the tender bow of her lip. "No need to tell him."

DAVID'S VISITOR

There was little to occupy David at the house—the occasional leaky tap, a door hinge in need of oiling—so he turned his attention to the books he had been meaning to read, a list that had lengthened each year of his working life. He began on the light side with Mayle and Theroux but soon bored of their caricatured natives and assiduously timed one-liners. Mustering resolve he hefted Milton down from the shelf and stretched out on the sofa with the tome on his belly, remembering how poetry had once been his sole rebellion, Thomas and Auden high priests of liberalism, Neruda a plumed Latin god, Brodsky the prophet of some vodka-laced netherworld. *When I consider how my light is spent...* His eyelids grew heavy.

Roused by the drone of an unmuffled engine, he gazed on reflex toward the shuttered windows. Beyond them a motorcycle revved and then went dead. He heard footsteps on the gravel path, three rhythmic raps of the doorknocker, Madame Fermat stamping down the stairwell in her Alsatian clogs. He heard as if from a great distance, at the bottom of a pit or deep within a cave. The afternoon sun heaved its heat through the shutter chinks. He forced open his eyes.

The housekeeper stood backlit in the doorway, hands on hips, saying, "Someone for you."

He nudged the tome onto the seat cushion and padded toward the foyer thinking, whom have I forgotten to pay—the roofer, the plumber, the oncologist who rents out his backhoe? Half the village had entered his employ at one point or another, but the man who stood on the welcome mat was no one he recognized. Tall, unkempt, bearded, his dark eyes hinting at Eastern origins, he clutched a motorcycle helmet to his bluejeaned hip.

Before David could frame a greeting, the man strode forward and extended his hand for a shake. "Lieutenant Lebrun, *à votre service.*"

"David Crown—but I suppose you know my name."

"Your name, case number, a few particulars…" The lieutenant's gaze drifted. "Lionel told me you were a man of taste. *Elle est belle, eh?*" He gestured broadly then smacked his lips.

"So, you're a friend of Lionel?"

"We were in the Navy together, not long, but long enough to get on each other's nerves—that sort of friend."

"What brings you to Beautemps?"

"I'm here about your Arabs." He might have been talking about a pair of pullets.

"I'll have Madame Fermat bring you a coffee."

He waved the offer away. "What I have to say won't take a minute. Mixing with that element is a *mauvaise idée.* What do you know about these hoodlums, anyway?"

"Only what Lionel told me."

"Well, *I* know them." Chest thrust wide, he pointed a cocked thumb at his breastbone. "They hate Jews. They hate

France. They want to see this country burn."

"I'm neither political nor religious."

"Yet you stick your neck out. It's irrational."

"That may be, but what would happen if I didn't?"

The lieutenant thumped his helmet with a chafe-knuckled fist. "Who are you anyway, the Messiah? *Merde.* Bad enough we had to deal with that rabbi."

"Then he's all right?"

"Smoke inhalation. Had he gone back into that synagogue one more time the contents of his skull would have boiled and exploded like an egg left too long on the stove—that's what happens, you know."

David hadn't known and the thought turned his stomach.

"Good thing big brother confessed. The crime scene held no more clues than a crepe suzette."

David caught sight of Madame Fermat, half hidden by the staircase and pretending to dust.

"There's an expression young Arabs use," the lieutenant went on, "*feuj*—perhaps you've heard it?"

It sounded vaguely familiar, vaguely unsavory.

"They use it to describe anything that disgusts them: a lousy meal, a clogged drain, a bad smell… It means Jewish."

David felt his throat clench. "Hate language is nothing new."

"I'm no historian. If it were up to me, I'd throw your Arabs into *la Sante* and let them marinate for a few years—now there's a real prison."

David tried again to offer the visitor a coffee, and again he declined.

"You're not going to change your mind, are you?"

"Are you saying I can see them?"

"The kids' mother came to my office the other day. On something—pills? Horse? Says the father is threatening to leave if she lets her sons back into the house. The social worker's report reads like Dante's *Inferno*."

"It can't be easy for the boys."

"Lionel told me you were a bleeding heart. *Merde.*"

Lebrun promised to make the arrangements, gave David the number of his direct line, and told him to call in a few days. "Maybe you'll come to your senses by then," he said, not sounding particularly hopeful. He opened the door, and the foyer flooded with the golden light of early dusk. "How could anyone *not* love this country?" Audibly filling his lungs, he stood looking out over the fields.

"Thank you for coming by."

His eyes still probing the horizon, the lieutenant slowly shook his head. "You're a fool if you think it's going to make a damn bit of difference."

ROWENA AT THE CRIME SCENE

Call it morbid curiosity. Rowena wanted to see the firebombed synagogue, to see firsthand what David had described only in monosyllables.

"It might do you good to go back," she ventured, studying his expression for the least sign of resistance.

"A day out. I'll have Madame Fermat pack a picnic lunch." Taking off a frayed gardening hat, replacing it with a smooth new Panama, he drove her to the city.

As asphalt and concrete devoured the landscape she regretted having asked him to make the trip. He seemed relaxed enough, but the vein at his temple faintly pulsed. They arrived late morning in a premature heat, the sky more yellow than blue and the air scratchy with diesel fuel. David was quiet. Not quiet in the usual way, but so detached he might have been part of the scenery. On an unfamiliar street they left the car and walked along the sidewalk with their elbows knocking.

"Look, if you'd rather we go back…"

David, sounding too eager to accommodate, said, "We're here. In a moment you'll see it."

The building was standing but boards covered its windows, barricades rimmed its iron gate. A scaffold stood to one side and men in white coveralls crouched atop it, their hands moving like wiper blades across the smoke-grayed façade. Rowena approached as close as the barrier allowed.

"It doesn't seem too bad," she said.

"They hurled the bombs from the rear garden, that's where the bulk of the damage would have been done."

"Maybe we can have a look. There's bound to be someone inside."

David drew back a step. "It's been years since I last entered a synagogue. Not since I recited my *Haftorah,* some interminable rant from Leviticus that I learned by rote and understood not at all. My stomach was in knots, afraid I'd forget the words."

"That would be a torment in front of your whole family."

"No, just Miriam, rapt as a pillar of salt in the gallery wearing her Jacqueline Kennedy hat."

"She must have felt proud."

"It was a question of duty, of tradition. What she was feeling I haven't a clue. I would ask her, but…" He shrugged. "When it was over, when I'd finished my recitation, the rabbi took the Torah scrolls from the tabernacle and placed them in my arms. To hold the Torah is an honor—that's what my mother told me, but what did I know? Relief was all I felt."

"Don't be so hard on yourself. You were just a kid."

"There was a man here the day of the fire. Not the bombers but a bearded man, the rabbi apparently. Whether he was in the building or came running when the fire began,

I don't know. But he had no fear. He braved the flames to rescue the Torah scrolls. They meant more to him than his own life."

"But the Torah is just another book."

"Yes—no." His chin grazed the placket of his polo. "I'm hardly the person to say."

A pair of gendarmes strolled past, giving them a discreet once-over. David put on his English face—doughy, unreadable—and lowered the brim of his Panama. Having seen what she had come for, Rowena took his hand, and they marched like a retreating army down the street to the car. No burning omens called them back.

The Tenacity of Hatred

The juvenile wing of the prison was not so much ugly as null, the air stagnant and cloying with pine freshener. The elder of David's assailants, visibly on edge, was already seated in the visitation room at a metal table when the guard admitted David. The young man—Emile, he'd been told to call him—glanced his way but didn't offer a greeting.

He seated himself opposite the prisoner and extended a hand. "I'm David Crown. Thanks for agreeing to see me."

"Did I have a choice?" Emile replied, staring a moment at the hand before acquiescing to a limp shake. His eyes had lost their glint, rested in their sockets like dry pebbles.

The guard stifled a belch and posted himself at the door.

"I don't know what they told you, the authorities, but I had assumed this was voluntary. I thought you might want to talk."

"*Pas du tout.*"

"Emile, what happened that day at the synagogue…"

"If you're expecting to hear me say I'm sorry… "

In truth, David wasn't sure what he wanted to hear. "Perhaps if we just get to know each other."

"What do you want to know?"

"You. Your family. Your life."

"*Moi*, I'm no one. My family? They're not your business." A pause as the prisoner swatted a fly and flicked its remains onto the floor. "I told all that shit to the social worker, as if it matters."

The guard half turned, ground a fist into his palm. "*Cinq minutes.*"

They sat in silence, Emile soundlessly drumming on the table edge, and David grappling for a cipher, a smidgeon of wisdom. But it was the boy who spoke first. "You got something to say, say it."

"What I want is to tell you that your life can change course. That everything is still possible. One day, one misstep, needn't determine your future."

Emile gave a bitter little smile. "Future? There is no future for *mecs* like me."

"Look, I don't presume to know you, what you're up against. I just know that life gets away from a man. You think there's time, and then suddenly it has all passed you by." He blushed at his own transparency then squared his shoulders. "You and your brother will be out of here soon. If you want a fresh start, if you're man enough to reach for it, get in touch." He took a card from his wallet and handed it across the table.

Emile hesitated. "You some sort of Mother Teresa or something? Some *baba cool* with money to burn? Keep your charity."

"It's your brother I'm thinking about, damn it!" David paused to let his anger subside. "How long will he last on these streets? Don't wait to find out. Ring me up."

Opaque as clay, the boy pocketed the card. "Anything

else?"

David shook his head, and the prisoner yawned and lumbered to his feet.

"I bashed you around pretty good," he said with thinly veiled satisfaction. "People like you... you ask for it." He paused to study David's face—was he hoping to find scars?

"The offer stands."

The guard nudged the boy through the door and down a long, gray corridor. David loosened his collar—his throat might have been lined with steel wool—and stepped out, wanting only to find an exit.

ROWENA STRAYS

Rowena heard the station wagon drive off at dawn. Since David's incident she often awoke alone in the oversized bed, took breakfast alone, sifting aimlessly through her notes or writing letters home that she would abandon after a sentence or two.

David's mother, left to fend for herself, never left the chateau. She drifted through its passageways mystified, breathless before each closed door. She always seemed surprised to see Rowena, as if each meeting were their first. She was not in the habit of knocking.

"*Ah*, there you are!"

Rowena stood in the shower, working up a lather under the jet spray.

"I promised Davey I'd look in on you."

"Thoughtful."

Miriam was still wearing her pink silk bed jacket and Lana Turner slippers. She took a few steps forward on the nailhead heels. "He's gone out, you know." She stepped closer, and for a moment Rowena thought she might slip into the stall with her. To her relief the old woman detoured to the sink, inspected herself in the mirror, and adjusted the spit curls that framed her temples.

"I'll just rinse off."

"He's missed tea twice this week. Where do you suppose he goes?"

The very question Rowena had been wrestling with before Miriam's intrusion.

"Towel, dear?" She took one from the rack and held it out.

Rowena turned off the water and began toweling off.

"If you don't mind my asking, dear, what do you do all day?"

How many times had she already told Miriam she was writing a book?

"We see so little of you." Miriam pouted and a thousand tiny crinkles rimmed her painted mouth. "My late husband, Davey's father, kept a cot at his office. He worked so very hard. Davey's brother Barry takes after him: same business acumen, same take-charge attitude. But Davey… Davey has always been a little independent. He's the baby, you know."

"David is nearly fifty years old."

"He's been looking a tad jaded, Davey has."

She had been told of the assault but seemed more apt to attribute her son's moods to the weather.

"Such a sensitive boy, used to break out in hives."

"I'd better get dressed."

"Quite right, so had I." Miriam's hands rose to the level of her bosom in the manner of a soprano about to sing an aria. For a moment she stared down into the palms and her expression subtly altered, leaving her lips first limp then taut. "Do be a lamb and ring for my Lady of the Bedchamber."

"Excuse me?"

"I can hardly receive the Lord Chamberlain in these old

rags." With a toss of her silver-blue curls she turned to go.

"But Mrs. Crown—"

"Who said anything about a crown? The state opening of Parliament is months off."

Rowena trailed her into the bedroom and yanked open a curtain, flooding the room with sunlight. Miriam, her metallic tresses a nimbus, froze midway to the door. Between them a din of cicadas, a cacophony reason couldn't breach. Rowena studied Miriam's face but saw only the blank stare of dementia.

"I'll ring right now," she assured her.

At last the matron gave a measured nod, and chin erect marched out of the room with her high heels ringing. Rowena pulled on the shorts and tank top that had become her work clothes and crossed the corridor to the many-windowed room David had furnished with a leather-topped desk, filing cabinet, and overstuffed chaise lounge, the sort of office a writer dreams of—stately, silent. Each morning at eight sharp she would shut herself away and not emerge until evening.

But that day the room might have been a holding cell. She could not write, nor could she pretend that her scribbled notes amounted to anything more than pallid reflections on an era that revolted her, a heroine who evaded her, and her own inadequacies, which every day of her writing life became more self-evident.

From the tyranny of the empty page there is only one escape: to walk away. With equal parts stealth and abandon she let herself out a rear door.

Drawn by a burst of poppies on the horizon, she followed the winding driveway to the road, turned left and left again. The road became a dirt track; to either side sprawled groves of trees and sown fields. Normally she would have walked a stretch and circled back, but that day she detoured to a splintered wooden sign—*Privé*—and unlatched an iron gate. She passed a small stone cottage with a single chair on its porch and an outdated tractor parked alongside. Hearing hammer blows, she approached a three-walled shed, where Swijdendorp stood at a workbench with nails poking out from between his lips.

"Hand me that board," he said without looking at her.

She complied mechanically. The farmer set himself to the task with a grimace of concentration.

"Clamp."

"Look, I haven't come to apprentice. If you're busy…"

He rested his elbows on the workbench and looked at her, looked so intently she felt her face grow hot. "You must be bored," he said.

"No, I was intrigued… about trufficulture. You made it sound so compelling."

"It's hardly that." His gaze left her and drifted along the rows of staked and pruned saplings.

"I guess I'll be going."

"No need to dash off. Here—" He grabbed a crate and placed it on the dirt floor. "Sit down. I'm out of practice, but let's have a civil conversation." He went on with his work.

"What about?"

"This Mr. Crown of yours, I hear he's some kind of scion."

"You mean his family's mega stores? David has no hang-ups about it."

"So, he's keeping you?"

She stood up, overturning the crate. "David respects my independence. He's no sugar daddy, and I'm no—"

"Why do you blush? It's a sensible arrangement: You're nubile, he's rich."

"You *are* out of practice."

He set down his tools and turned the crate upright. He

clapped the dust from his hands. "Crown seems a decent enough fellow and less of a cliché than the other Brits in this town."

"Stop by the house sometime. The renovation's complete, David's been climbing the walls, and we could all use some company."

"Don't expect me. What could I possibly find to say to people like that?"

More curious than offended, she took a few steps along the shed wall amid a plethora of hoes and spades and bundled chicken wire. Her back prickled. She glanced over a shoulder and found him studying her as one might a road sign or weather vane. "What are you looking at?"

The farmer, inscrutable within the frame of his lank blonde bowl of hair, positioned a nail. "I just noticed that you are entirely covered with skin. I should like to see you nude—but you're blushing again. How inconvenient. Let me get you a glass of water."

She veered and stamped past him out of the shed, through the gate, and did not stop until the road divided them. She paused in the shade while the heat left her cheeks then started up the driveway, telling herself nothing had happened. Nothing at all.

A CRY FOR HELP

David loped through the chateau's halls, pausing again and again before the door of Rowena's office but not daring to knock. Nearly lunchtime, not that he had an appetite. He could smell Madame Fermat's *coq au vin* simmering in the kitchen. Restless, he stepped outside, surveyed the grounds, which were hilly and unkempt, and knelt to pick a few random weeds.

Inside, the telephone rang.

"I'll get it," David called in the housekeeper's direction. Madame had stepped onto the rear patio to shake out the feather duster that seldom left her chapped and harried hands.

Sidestepping her with a polite nod, he entered the library, closed the door behind him, and picked up the nearest handset.

"*C'est vous*, Crown? Lebrun here." The lieutenant spoke above a din of raised voices and slamming doors. "We didn't have a chance to talk at the facility. It's not easy, your first time inside."

"Is this about Emile?" Since his visit to the prison, David had thought of little else. "I don't suppose he has requested an encore?"

"It's not Emile I'm calling about. The kid brother, Rashid, has started a hunger strike. No list of demands, just some claptrap about discrimination. It hasn't caught on, but he won't back down."

"Where do I come in?"

"He's asking to talk to you. Kid's smart—they're dangerous, the smart ones. He knows how to get attention, but I'd rather he bitch to you than to the media. Human rights types would have a heyday."

"What if his claim were legitimate?"

"I'll pretend I didn't hear that, Crown. Hundreds of kids pass through our facility and don't lodge a single complaint. Rashid is testing the boundaries, *c'est tout*."

David, having taken the copper's measure, kept his doubts to himself. "And Emile?"

"He's been moved to another cell block. Bad influence, that one."

David paced along the bookshelves with one hand skimming bindings, as if to absorb their contents through osmosis. If only he were a wiser man, a proper role model. "I may be no influence at all, but I'll hear the boy out."

"Nobody's twisting your arm."

"Nobody has to."

"I wouldn't blame you for washing your hands of these *petits misérables*."

David stifled a sigh. "I'd blame myself."

"What seminary did they wash your brain in?" The lieutenant laughed at his own joke, if laughter his gruff, toneless cackle could be called. "Tomorrow, then."

LIONEL VANQUISHES A PAPER CUP

Summer had always been Lionel's season of preference, but this year the hordes of tourists wore a decidedly aggressive mien. There were more Germans, more Russians, more Eastern Europeans. They did not stay long—all were headed for the coast—but their dour expressions and hideous aftershave cast a pall that would not lift until evening, when the sound of cowbells and heavy metal signaled a change of mood. Commuters shed their suits and dove headlong into chlorinated pools; widows took down their laundry from the balcony rail; the leisured drifted onto patios for a second cocktail.

Attuned to Beautemps' perennial cycles, Lionel noted the seasonal increase of litter, worse this year. The sight of it never failed to incense him. In this case, a discarded paper cup left to drift on the breeze. He chased the cup, not in an obvious way, which would have looked undignified, but with persistence. The pursuit took him off course, down a tatty side street that had once housed the village's only known prostitute, into an alley spattered with chicken droppings, and along a wall collapsing to rubble. The cup rose and fell, always a step ahead of him. No longer a mere receptacle but a metaphor for ruin, it teased and mocked and would not let him be. Abandoning caution he lunged forward with both arms extended and at last pocketed his prey.

Satisfied, he wiped the soles of his shoes against a low curb and was about to head for home when a folded leaflet, carried by the breeze, collided with his ankle. As he bent to retrieve it, he caught sight of old Gaultier. One of the boules crowd, brittle remnant of *la France profonde*, the geezer glanced warily in his direction and then quickly away. Lionel scanned the leaflet's heading, *"Immigation Zéro,"* a slogan he had heard bandied about by xenophobes interviewed on the evening news. "Keep France for the French, send them back…"

"I think you dropped this." Lionel held the soiled newsprint sheets out to Gaultier, who snarled, hesitated, and finally balled the papers into his black beret and walked away.

Lionel arrived home to find David Crown, freshly shaven, more razor-burnt than bruised, shuffling his feet on the doormat. "Afraid I'm late for that game of chess," he said.

"That was last week. I wondered what had happened to you."

Lionel unlocked the front door with the original latchkey, a relic, unwieldy by the day's standards but solid in his hand. The scent of his wife's perfume greeted him, though she had left for work early in the day and had yet to return. Following its trail, he padded across the living room rug and waved David into an armchair.

The Englishman brought a hand to his chin, as if to stroke a nonexistent beard. "I seem to have lost track of time."

"I couldn't help but notice your windscreen. Didn't the glass man phone you?"

"He did, if I remember correctly."

"You made an appointment to have it replaced?"

"I'd need to check my diary."

A sudden breeze jangled the shutters. Lionel got up and walked to a nearby window; through its pane he could see the river and beyond it ordered fields, one aligned with the next. "It's all changing. I'm the first generation not to till the soil, yet this land holds me. The tourists could leave tomorrow and no one in Beautemps would mourn them. The European Union could come apart at its seams. I would take my few miserable canoes out of the water and plant some vines, like that hermit Swijdendorp. There's a man of sense. Doesn't answer to anyone—that's the ideal, isn't it?"

"Indeed."

Lionel turned and found David beside him, gazing out at the same vista. "Ready for that game of chess?" he asked.

"Can't stay, I'm afraid. That friend of yours—"

"Lebrun?"

"Lebrun called this morning about the younger of the brothers, about Rashid. He's refusing to eat."

"So?" Leave it to his old Navy chum to stir the pot. "What does he expect you to do about it?"

"The boy is asking to see me."

"David, David… why get mixed up in this? Consider the consequences. Let's say the kid does himself in, then what? Either the gang or a relative comes after you—doesn't matter what your motives were, they must find someone to blame, someone upon whom to wreak revenge."

"Sounds like a bad film noir."

"*Exactement.* Life in the *banlieues c'est ça*, a dark violent cliché with nothing to redeem it, the same senseless story repeated again and again… and when the lights come up, you're left with a sickness in your gut. You want to feel sorry for these people, you want to fix things, but there's a wall between us and them—a wall of hatred. What makes you think you can get around it? Christ himself couldn't."

They sat a long time in silence, each chained to a separate wound. David rose and steered toward the door, pausing a moment alongside Lionel's armchair to lay a hand on his slouched shoulder.

"You've been a good friend, Lionel."

"Don't forget about the windscreen."

The Englishman let himself out. Lionel watched from the window as he strode briskly toward the Volvo, seeming, if not his old self, a normal enough man.

SECOND THOUGHTS

Those gargoyles never did find a place on the chateau's roof.

More than once David thought about getting out a ladder and installing them, but when one day he unwrapped them and looked into their vacant eyes, his stomach clenched. He covered them back up. What use had he for a waterspout, anyway? The roof was drier than a camel's hoof.

Wondering at her *patron's* folly, Madame Fermat found an empty corner in the garage and shut the useless creatures away.

SCARS

Rashid had been transferred to the prison infirmary by the time David arrived for their scheduled meeting. The boy was still refusing to eat. As many times as the doctors inserted an IV needle into his arm, he would pull it out again, tearing the skin, bloodying himself. The doctors had no choice but to bind his wrists.

David entered the ward, which was half empty, and scanned the iron beds. At the far end lay a compact figure, lean, curly-haired, with a finely chiseled face whose cheeks resembled a tic-tac-toe board.

"What's the matter, mister, am I too pretty for you?" He spoke English, spoke it well for a Frenchman.

"Mind if I sit down?"

He upturned a palm, as much of a gesture as his vinyl wrist restraints allowed.

"I suppose your brother, Emile, told you about our meeting."

"Yeah, he thought you were an asshole."

David broke into peals of laughter, one endless release of nerves. Leaning forward in the iron chair, clutching his ribs, he ventured, "And you? What do you think?"

"*Moi?* " A dimple peeked out from his grid of scars. "I think you're sort of old and smell of money."

David had arrived intending to instill the norms of polite, lawful society, but instead he nearly rent his sides laughing. "Forgive me, I haven't laughed like this since... since..."

"Go ahead, man, it's *halal.*"

David wiped tears from his eyes.

Having demonstrated his proficiency in the Queen's English, Rashid reverted to French. "My brother doesn't know I'm meeting you. Lebrun promised not to tell—Lebrun's all right for a *keuf*—so don't you either."

"Agreed."

A prisoner across the aisle called in a stage whisper, "Anyone got a joint?"

"You're right," David went on, "about my having had a few advantages in life."

"It's obvious, an English *mec* with straight teeth."

"A family friend specialized in orthodontics." David heard the note of apology in his own voice. "Best not to place too much stock in appearances. We may not be so very different, you and I."

"Sure, mister, just don't expect sympathy."

"Agreed. I was only saying…"

A brawny orderly entered wheeling a gurney, upon which lay a black man with a bandaged head. "They fucked him up pretty bad," said Rashid, raising his head from the pillow only to flop down again like a rag doll.

"I must be tiring you." David looked from the battered man to the starving boy and felt the same impotent outrage that welled up in him each time he scanned the newspaper headlines or heard Tony Blair address Parliament.

"What's the matter, mister, late for a golf game?"

"I don't play golf."

Rashid's bound hand strained toward him. "I don't blame you for wanting to get the hell out. This place sucks. No one sees, but I'm treated real bad here. They won't let me live and won't let me die."

"What does Lebrun say?"

"That I should have thought about that before I threw the bombs."

"He's got a point." A guard lumbered slowly up the aisle, heading their way. "Look, we don't have much time. Survive this and you'll be a free man in a few months. Just survive."

"Survive for *what?*" He was asking David for a reason to live, nothing less. Somewhere beneath the wounds and feigned indifference there was fight, the stubborn, unrelenting drive to matter.

"I don't have all the answers, but life has surprised me sometimes and been more forgiving than anyone has a right to expect. Survive and I'll be here when you get released. We'll figure something out."

The guard caught David's eye and signaled with his chin toward the exit. The Englishman rose to go.

"Sure, mister," said Rashid and turned away.

David would have liked to tousle his curls. He looked

so small, so lost, in the iron bed. The guard peeled open a curtain, and a beam of light streamed across the bedclothes onto the boy's face. His scars glowed like neon.

CHECKMATE

Ratty from a summer cold, Lionel moped in the front garden. Laura had gone to the next *département* to spend the weekend with her parents, leaving him an herbal remedy from the Chinese chemist and half a dozen pure butter croissants.

Their neighbors, the Boncoeurs, had left on holiday, forsaking their aged spaniel, Brioche. The dog walker drove up on a scooter with an assortment of leashes coiled about her arms. She greeted him with a nod, let herself in the gate, and emerged moments later crawling backwards, trying to lure the dog out with a handful of grainy biscuits. Lionel made a beeline to the kitchen for a cube of cheese.

"*Tenez, mademoiselle*," he called, extending the tidbit over the hedge. "I know Brioche, he's a connoisseur. You'll only offend his sensibilities."

The old spaniel began to caper like a puppy, and the walker slipped the leash about his neck and led him away. Lionel lingered at the foot of the garden, watching the dog's wagging tail with the satisfaction of a man who's done his part. As he turned with no greater ambition than to reoccupy his seat, David Crown, softly whistling, strolled up the path.

"I'll get the chess board," Lionel said and felt his old enthusiasm return.

"I looked for you at the river," the usual venue of their matches. "The attendant said you weren't well."

"I'm well enough."

Before long they were settled at a picnic table with a lawn umbrella swaying above their heads, the board between them, and brimming glasses of iced coffee growing fogged at their fingertips. The Frenchman took the two kings in his closed fists and held them out.

"Are those blisters on your hand, David?"

"Oh those. I thought I'd plant a garden."

"Hobby of yours?"

"Don't know the first thing about it," he admitted.

"Bachelor buttons, hollyhocks, that sort of thing?"

"Pergolas, fountains, topiary… haven't given it much thought, but why not?" David sat back in his chair, staring out over the hills with an unfocused look. "Why not?" he repeated, warming to the idea.

He tapped Lionel's right fist.

"*Blanc*," Lionel said and replaced the pieces on their squares.

David, distracted even before the game began, nudged a pawn forward two squares. "The landscape has lain neglected for years, a haven for stinging nettles. I went to a plant nursery and the proprietor set me up with everything I need for a complete overhaul."

Lionel mirrored the Englishman's sortie. "Knowing you, the village will soon have its own Versailles."

David laughed, which made him look for a moment like a big loose-lipped child. "Nothing quite so grand as that." He fiddled with a rook. "Do you think Leclerc would mind bringing me a riding mower from the city? I can't seem to find one closer to home."

"Consider it done. I'll have him call you Monday morning."

As the game proceeded David grew reckless, whether from bravado or lack of attention Lionel could not judge. His casualties steadily mounted.

"Lebrun tells me your young friend is back on solid food," Lionel said, watching a path open toward the

Englishman's queen. "You might want to take him some baklava. There's an Arab baker near the prison."

"The guards dissect everything." He draped an arm along the chair back and gazed again toward the horizon.

"The game, David. You're not concentrating."

"Sorry. You were saying?"

"The baklava. I'll talk to Lebrun. And I hear the boy's into poetry—a shared interest, *n'est-ce pas?*"

"Who'd have thought?"

They played a round in silence, David venturing defenseless onto uncharted ground, and Lionel exploiting his blind spots. *"Bof,* how can I enjoy trouncing you if you won't even glance at the board now and then?"

"So, what's new in the village?" A routine question, posed as Lionel carried off David's castle.

"I've been meaning to talk to you about Swijdendorp— between us, *compris?*"

The Englishman looked up from his pieces and nodded.

"Seems he's managed to grow some truffles."

"He said he hadn't."

"David, David... do you know nothing of human nature? Of course he didn't tell anyone. A man with truffles had better know how to keep his mouth shut. Where there are truffles, there are poachers, and that's the *Hollandais'* problem. He's found their tracks." Brioche arrived back from his walk with belly grazing the sidewalk and his minder in tow. *"Ça va, mademoiselle?"*

David made a sloppy move.

"You'd do well to guard your queen," Lionel chided. He maneuvered his knight through a maze of pieces and took her.

"That's too bad about Swijdendorp. Can anything be done?"

"A few of us have been patrolling with him, but we're talking about two hundred hectares. We could use another pair of eyes." He jumped his knight into range of David's king. "Check."

"Swijdendorp seems a decent sort. Count me in." David improvised a defense but could not long escape the inevitable.

"Checkmate."

The Englishman, looking relieved to be done with it, angled his chair away from the table and stretched out his legs.

"Once a man loses his *femme*," murmured Lionel, reflecting on the game but laying bare his very heart, "he's done for."

His friend bolted upright, as if awakened by lightning.

"Let me get you a pastis."

"Another time." Before Lionel could insist, David was halfway to the gate. "Do let me know about Swijdendorp," said the Englishman in the *all-for-one and one-for-all* tone Lionel associated with old swashbucklers. "Can't let a good man be pillaged." He walked off at a brisk clip, and his whistling resumed. The tune sounded vaguely nautical— Gilbert and Sullivan?

Lionel transferred the chess pieces to their wooden box, clutched the board to his ribs, and padded toward the house. Midway, squinting, he stole a look at the sky. A cloud floated across his field of vision, mimicking in its crescent-like form the flaky golden crust of a pure butter croissant. He could almost taste it.

PARADISE REGAINED

When David lost sight of Lionel, he had one desire and one only. He raced for his estate car, turned back toward the

Vie Dorée, parked, hurdled the doorstep, entered at a trot and bounded up the stairs two at a time—had the house been on fire, he could not have upped his pace. The door to Rowena's office stood ajar and on the threshold stood Rowena, barefoot, her head bowed over a sheaf of notes.

"Spare a moment?"

She gave a shrug and stepped through the office door. He followed too closely, clipping her on the heel. When he reached down to soothe the offended foot, she gave a little hop and waved him into the chair opposite her desk.

"You're cross with me."

"Should I be?"

"How's your writing coming along?"

"Is that what you've come to talk about?"

"No, of course not, but I thought I'd ask. We've seen so little of each other these past days."

"Who's complaining? I don't expect to be entertained."

He got up, circled the desk. She had filed the notes and her empty hands worried the straps of her tank top. Her shoulders, wary little blades, had a blush to them.

"Forgive me, I haven't been myself. There were things I needed to sort out."

"I don't suppose I've been much help."

"Don't say that. What could you, what could anyone, have done?"

"Anything you had asked, but you don't ask. You don't ask for a darned thing."

Stung, he circled away. She kept on fussing with her straps, revealing contrasting ribbons of skin the sun had not touched, fragile white arrows pointing to the haven from which he had been exiled. "I couldn't bear to have you see me weak."

"Stop trying to be some hero out of a book. You've been that to me, my white knight, but it's okay to fall off your steed now and then."

"Red Rose, proud Rose, sad Rose of all my days!" Nothing short of Yeats could have risen to the moment, but still Rowena kept a distance. "I'm here now," he said, aligning both palms on the desk edge. "I'm back."

She exhaled audibly, the closest he had heard her come to a sigh. A single tear beaded on her lashes and clung. Gazing past him she walked to the window and opened the shutters. "Look at it out there, like a postcard."

"The way we both envisioned it. Only it's real, it's ours."

"No, it will never be ours."

He approached from behind and planted his lips on the wing of her back. A hint of lavender wafted from her nape. "Do you miss working at the library?"

"Does a slave miss her manacles?"

"Do you miss our lovemaking?"

The blush spread to her neck, crept like a pilgrim to the hollow of her breasts. As if to shake it off, she veered, answering him with searching hands and a kiss so deep it made him buckle.

FROM THE BALLS

David donned his Panama, whistled a few bars from *Peter Pan,* and paced the foyer, waiting for Rowena to finish dressing. The picnic lunch Madame Fermat had prepared sat at his feet in a wicker basket. The day was perfect, dry with just a hint of breeze. In a moment Rowena would race down the staircase and off they would go, carefree as truants. And then lieutenant Lebrun was on the phone, intruding like a storm cloud.

"C'est vous, Crown? Have I caught you at a bad moment?"

Hearing the lieutenant's hacksaw voice, David felt his throat tighten. "Is Rashid all right?"

"*Merveilleux.* Your little friend is back in his cell, happy as a clam. Visitation days are Wednesday and Sunday, afternoons between two and four, no exceptions."

Caught off-guard by the breadth of his own relief, David could only stammer, "I'll be there this Sunday."

"I'd tread lightly if I were you. These hoods from the *banlieues* charm your socks off and then cut your heart out with a scimitar."

"May I take him something, a gift?"

"Nothing liquid, nothing sharp. Anything else will be run through an X-ray."

"How about books?"

"All these kids read anymore is comic books. I suppose a paperback would be okay—in French. No porn, no Noam Chomsky, no ranting imams…"

David was making a concerted effort not to dislike Lebrun.

"No *Mein Kampf,* no Robert Faurisson."

"How about poetry?"

"*Mother Goose* maybe," the lieutenant mocked. "Really, Crown, you and your romantic notions…"

The day's outing forgotten, David scanned the few French-language volumes in his library and decided on T. S. Eliot, Dylan Thomas, and Lord Byron. When, the following Sunday, he arrived at the prison, a gloved guard thumbed through the books, turned them spine up and gave a shake, then fed them one by one into the tunnel-like X-ray. As they emerged out the other end, a second guard signaled David to retrieve them. They felt warm in his hands like loaves not long out of the oven.

A third guard blocked the entry to the visitation room and patted him down. "Back again?" he asked absently.

David passed into a large hospital-green cubicle filled with weeping mothers. Rashid waited in a corner seated on a plastic chair, elbows on knees, fingers drumming. He wore the baggy casual clothing fashionable among urban youth—dropped-crotch pants, oversized t-shirt—and worried the plastic identity bracelet on his wrist.

The boy half stood. "Join the party."

David would have liked to lead him past the guards, past the walls, and out into the summer air. He looked so bony, so bereft, in his clownish garb. "I thought you might want to read something, help the time pass."

"Cool." The prisoner took the books, clutched them for a moment to his heart, and laid them on a side table. "Poetry rocks, not the stuff they make us read at school but Dylan Thomas, D. H. Lawrence... Those *mecs* wrote from their balls."

David, more tickled by the remark than he thought it proper to acknowledge, said, "Yes, the work does have a bracing masculinity about it. I'll bring you a Lawrence next time."

"Nothing but Spiderman and Astérix in the prison library. Smell like puke—everything here smells like puke."

One of the weeping women cried out, *"Courage, mon fils!"*

There were questions David might have posed—Why does a fifteen-year old boy try to burn down a synagogue? Why does that same boy then sit amiably conversing with a Jew?—but instead he touched his fingertips to Rashid's forehead and asked, "Touch of fever?" The boy's flushed face contrasted starkly with the pallor of his neck and arms.

"There's always something going around."

"Have they given you anything for it—a flu shot, a pill?"

The prisoner shot David a *what-planet-are-you-from*

look. "In this place best thing for a man's health is to be invisible."

"You'll be out soon. In the meantime, it's a roof over your head and a chance to think."

Rashid leaned in close and lowered his voice. "They make fun of me, mister, insult my mother. What am I supposed to do? Say yeah, you're right, my mother *is* a whore, thanks for reminding me?"

"It's just words."

The boy thumped his chest with a clenched fist. "It's my honor."

"People like that, they're not worth risking your freedom for. Ignore them."

"Why do they always win?" His voice swelled with the impotent rage that is the undertone of prison life. "They've got the jobs, the houses, the women…"

Not for the first time David scavenged his paltry store of aphorisms for a nugget of wisdom. "Okay, so life isn't fair. That doesn't mean you can't make a go of it, practice a profession, and find a wife."

"Who would marry me with this face?" You think I'm blind?"

"No, but love is."

"You believe that hot air? How about your woman—would she love you if you lived in a sty and had nothing to give her but promises? Get real, mister."

"*Though lovers be lost love shall not.*"

"So you know Thomas. Even poets talk shit sometimes. If the *mec* believed his own words, why did he go and drink himself to death?"

Time was up and a dead poet had had the last word.

Rashid lumbered to his feet, took the books, and allowed himself to be herded back to the cellblock. David watched his narrow, slouching form recede down a gray corridor, watched a guard open an iron door, watched the door close. He turned to go.

"Why so glum?" Lebrun, the person David least wanted to see at that moment. There was something staged about his entrance, a precisely timed second act. A line of mothers filed past them, trailing tears and *eau de toilette*.

"I'm concerned about Rashid." He stole a last glance down the corridor, deserted now and crisscrossed by shadows. "Can't you tell your men to ease up on him?"

The lieutenant, off-duty, daubed the blood from a shaving nick. "This is a correctional facility, not a summer camp."

"What do you hope to correct through humiliation and brutality? The guards are no better than the prisoners."

"Watch how you talk about my men."

"If you would just listen to Rashid—"

"Watch it, Crown, eh?" Lebrun, his breath hot, jaw twitching, squared his stance. "I don't have to listen to some wimp *biftec* insult my men."

"I'm only suggesting—"

"You got a suggestion, write to the ombudsman. *Brutal*, my men? You know your way out."

ULTIMATUM

It had been a bad day at the *mairie*—the oscillating fan out of service, secretary called away for jury duty, land developers jockeying for permits... Made worse by the unexpected appearance of his old Navy chum, Jacques Lebrun.

Lebrun (whom no one called Jacques) had always been a figure of some ambivalence in Lionel's life, someone he admired and yet held at arm's length, unnerved by the obduracy of the man's beliefs—not that these were so different from Lionel's own. Neither had had a radical phase; both had served in the military. But there any similarity ended.

The lieutenant stormed into the room like a Hussar at the charge. "If it isn't the Arabs it's the English! Telling us how to live in our own country, demanding justice—justice for everyone but us French."

He could only have been referring to David Crown. "*Du calme*, Lebrun." Already preparing a defense, Lionel braced for the next sortie.

"I won't have some toffee-nosed Brit calling my men brutes. I won't stand for it. Who does he think he is, Winston Churchill?"

"The war's over."

"Don't be naïve, *mon pote*. The real war, *jihad*, the war our children will be left to fight, and their children after them, has barely begun."

"I don't know about any of that. I'm just mayor of a village." Lionel waved his visitor toward an armchair.

"Stop being such a pussy." The lieutenant, still palsied with ire, continued to pace. "You may live in Toyland, but you read the papers."

"This isn't about politics but friendship. I like David. If it makes him feel better to spend time in that stinking prison with some mixed-up kid, what harm is there in it?"

"Not *you* too! Our juvenile justice system is among the most progressive in the world."

"And our prisons among the most overcrowded."

"Next you'll be quoting chapter and verse from the International Convention of the Rights of the Child. Granted, we fall short. You think these kids' housing blocks smell any better? You think David's little hood is going to be any safer on the outside? The good ones get preyed upon by the bad." The cop crumpled into a chair and exhaled like a life raft deflating.

Lionel would have liked to disagree with him, but everything he had read, rife with war stories and body counts, pointed to the same dire prognosis. Who but a diehard like his old chum would throw himself into a losing battle day after day?

Lebrun glanced at his wristwatch. "I've got to get back. Some clueless bureaucrat from the ministry is stopping in for a photo op."

"You're a good man, Lebrun."

"So is your Englishman." The cop backhanded the chair with his ungainly rack of knuckles. "Pain in the ass."

"Prince of impossible causes."

"A prince he may be," said Lebrun, mustering a fresh head of steam, "but he had better watch his mouth. One more slur against my men and his goodwill mission is over, *compris?*"

DAVID PONDERS REPRODUCTION

As summer neared its peak Beautemps' canopy hung heavy with apricots, grapes and figs, more than could be harvested. Ripe fruits lay everywhere. With what gusto David pulled on his gardening gloves! The grounds of the chateau sprawled derelict: trees unpruned, flowerbeds choked with weeds, terraces fallen, and the hedges mined with nettles. A more experienced gardener might have felt cowed, but David set about the task as if to dance a jig. He had bought himself a spade, hoe and wheelbarrow. The riding mower was due to arrive within the week. He wore a hat left behind in the shed, its woven brim fraying, and billowing about his legs a favorite pair of shapeless linen shorts.

He began with the kitchen garden, pulling clumps of grass and weeds from the sketchily defined rows, turning over the earth. Madame Fermat stepped out onto the rear patio to shake her feather duster. Pretending not to watch him, she mused aloud, "The *misère* people endure to avoid hiring a gardener." She pirouetted and reentered the house, leaving a dust cloud to float about his head.

Undeterred, David dragged a bag of fertilizer from the shed and applied it generously to the neglected beds. He retrieved a second bag and a third, spreading the fertilizer around the roots of the chateau's several dozen fruit trees, then set about pruning. He breathed deeply of the still air, which held the musk of fermenting grapes. Drunk without raising a glass, he capered along the hedgerow wielding his shears.

"Enjoying yourself?" Miriam, deadpan behind her rhinestone sunglasses, inspected his handiwork.

"Never knew I had green fingers, did you?"

"Well, dear, you didn't get them from me. My victory garden was a second Blitz, carrots the size of fallen teeth— your father hated carrots."

"I'll just finish up."

Her lips twisted in a grin. "A century should do it."

"Then I've found my life's work."

He expended a week of frenzied effort, pausing only to apply lineament to his sore muscles. Rowena, a believer in projects, made frequent appearances at her office window to spur him on. "*Tote that barge, lift that bale...*" He whistled the tune, wishing she would descend from her bower and roll with him among the various soil amendments. Only once did he succeed in luring her down and leading her to the shed on the pretext of retrieving a rake. There was a teasing sway to her gait that he couldn't fail to notice.

"I've a notion to ravish you."

She melted obligingly into his hands. They teetered unzipped among an assortment of burlap sacks with rough fibers grazing their skin, and their tongues soothing the rubbed places. In his fantasies he had choreographed this dance a hundred times. He maneuvered her toward the workbench, already picturing her rump laid bare atop the knotty pine slab. She stepped out of her panties and handed them to him, virginal cotton briefs the color of daffodils. He deposited them in the straw hat. She climbed onto the bench unbidden, arrayed herself there like a gift without its wrappings.

And then a shadow dissected his field of vision: Madame Fermat, inches from the shed, taking a handful of Miriam's chocolate-covered cherries from her apron pocket and wolfing them down.

He covered Rowena with the first thing that came to hand, a grease-stained tarpaulin, and bundled her to the window. The wanton smile left her face. Breathing in heaves they knelt side by side at the sill watching the housekeeper lick her lips, her fingers, and light up a filterless cigarette.

By the start of week two David's back gave out and he lay in bed with a hot water bottle between his shoulder blades, thumbing back issues of *Jardin Practique*. Miriam gave her recipe for chicken soup to the housekeeper, who rendered it Gallic with the addition of basil, garlic and lavish spills of olive oil. David dredged the bottom of the bowl with a crust of bread. Despite the pain radiating up both sides of his spine, he could not shake his euphoria. Every patch of wall, every object lay bathed in sunlight; the air wafted fragrant, as if the garden had followed him indoors. He resolved to add another dozen trees to the grove, perhaps a gazebo. He reached for his straw hat and caressed its frayed brim. Tomorrow, without fail, he would take up his spade and begin anew.

Rowena stopped in at intervals, her bedside manner decidedly crisp. "Fermat keeps talking about someone named

Durand, an old gardener looking for work. Couldn't you use a hand?"

"I'm managing on my own, thank you."

"But your back—"

"It's fine now," he fibbed.

She circled him with a wary eye. "You don't look much better than those trees out there. Have you noticed the way they're losing their leaves?"

"Yes, well." He had heard that rural gardeners conversed with devas and sowed by the cycles of the moon; hire this Durand fellow and soon he would be pinning fetishes to the beanpoles. "I'll call the plant nursery."

As David's back mended he sat at the bedroom window looking out over his green and yellow and increasingly brown five hectares, straining to understand the peculiar intelligence that forms the anatomy of plants and gives them life. He imagined, albeit inaccurately, the meeting of seed and soil, the hidden inception, the germination, which, in the end, left him thinking of the child he never had. His wife couldn't conceive. They spoke briefly of adoption—in ideological terms, never with longing or hope—then lapsed into the dim sufficiency that characterized the last years of their marriage. They lost their leaves. On an impulse he pulled himself upright, hobbled to the door of Rowena's office, and opened it. Her gaze was slow to leave the computer screen. He approached by inches, feeling the pain shoot up his flanks with each step. He braced against her desk. "Could you— might we—shall we have a baby?"

"Are you delirious?" was all she said.

LIONEL DROPS THE RHODES

A mid-season heat wave blew in from Africa. One scorcher of a day, Lionel found Cecil and Hedy Rhodes'

BMW stopped alongside the road not far from the *hypermarché*. A front tire had gone flat. The Rhodes carried no spare. Deirdre Griffith, a sight in leopard-skin capris, accompanied them. There were no fewer than thirty bags of groceries in the trunk.

"Give us a lift, old boy?" Cecil said, his face the color of a stop sign.

Had it not been for a punctured tire, the mayor might never have formed more than the sketchiest impression of the Rhodes. Cecil, with his gelled hair and veiny nose seldom left the driving range. Hedy, the friendlier of the two, an aging coquette, once tried to lure him to a hotel on the pretext of "needing advice." The couple, self-appointed social directors of the foreign enclave, rarely mixed with the French and did not deign to learn their language. Indeed, the longer they sojourned in Beautemps, the more fiercely Britannic they seemed to become.

Leclerc was at the wheel of the municipal van. Lionel wedged the shopping bags to either side of David's riding mower (fresh from the showroom) and settled the passengers on the rear seat. His intention was to take the threesome to a nearby village where a friend owned a tire shop and then back to their stranded car. Deirdre, leaning forward, her breath clammy on his neck, said, "Russ had a blow-out just last week. You'd think they paved the roads with nails."

That France boasts one of the best road systems in the world, any fool knows, but Lionel said nothing. Cecil made a guttural sound as if to call pigs. "Stop your moaning," chided Hedy, lighting up an imported cigarette. Then to Lionel, "How's the canoe business? I've been meaning to stop by and have a paddle."

"The outlook for tourism has been good this year," the mayor replied in English, which he spoke poorly and Leclerc not at all. Lionel felt obliged to translate for him. *"Du vent,"* the driver muttered, waving the remark off.

"Just what our village needs," Hedy moaned, "more tourists."

"You are welcome," responded Lionel, having misconstrued the remark but determined to remain cordial. Leclerc turned to him with lifted eyebrows and he repeated the exchange in French.

Hedy sat back with a sigh. "Say something," she chided her husband, and the two began to bicker.

"That mower looks a high-ticket item," Deirdre broke in.

"French don't care how they spend our money. Tax everything but the air."

With little else to occupy him, Lionel found himself eavesdropping. Leclerc had run out of small talk hours ago and it would have seemed rude to turn on the radio. Besides, he told himself, these were his constituents; did he not have a duty to understand them, if only to keep them at bay? It wasn't long before Deirdre started in again.

"Russ and I are thinking of taking a folk dancing class."

"Gawd," rejoined Hedy, "it's so embarrassing watching one's compatriots go native. Cecil had a boules phase when we first arrived."

"Don't remind me."

"But it's so dull this season—no cocktails, no picnics…"

Cecil gave another grunt.

"We're losing our sense of community," said Hedy. "The new arrivals are a different class."

"Not all of them," Deidre countered. "How about David Crown? Haven't seen him in yonks."

"No loss. He's become such a whinger."

"I thought you fancied him?"

Hedy laughed. "Hardly, darling. He seemed a nice

enough chap at first, then some Arab ruffles his feathers and suddenly he's got a grudge against the whole world."

"What sort of name is Crown?"

"The rich ones change their names."

"Never did take to the girlfriend," said Cecil. "Don't suppose she's of the same persuasion?"

Lionel had heard enough. Changing course, Leclerc headed for home with his foot heavy on the accelerator. The Rhodes could sort out their own tires. The Rhodes could bloat at the bottom of *La Manche*, for all Lionel cared.

SPEAKING IN CODE

When David next visited the prison, a volume of D. H. Lawrence tucked beneath an arm, bag of baklava in hand, he was ushered to a private room, windowless, not much larger than a broom closet.

"You'll be more comfortable in here."

Moments later, Rashid entered and took the one remaining seat. "This Lebrun's idea? Knowing him the room is probably bugged." David was about to reassure the boy, when he winked and broke into an ironic smile.

"We'll speak in code."

"Good one, mister." Despite his apparent levity, Rashid scanned the woodwork. "They're cagey, these *keufs.*"

David placed his offerings on the table. "For you."

"You remembered," the boy said, beginning to skim the volume of verse. "*The space of the world is immense,*" he read aloud, "*before me and around me. If I turn quickly, I am terrified, feeling space surround me.*"

"*Like a man in a boat on very clear, deep water, space frightens and confounds me.*"

Rashid looked up in surprise.

"I've always loved that poem. I grew up alongside the

Thames in a place called Henley."

"Did you have a boat?"

"Not growing up but later—my wife liked to sail. I never found the time." This seemed suddenly sad to David, even tragic, and his mood took on the sterile, stifling atmosphere of the prison.

"Bummed about something?"

"No—well, actually."

"Girlfriend problems, I bet. There's a look guys get when their woman's giving them grief. You've got it bad, mister."

"Call me David."

"You've got that kicked look."

"Perhaps. We did have a sort of—"

"Sort of? Bet she really slayed you, didn't she? Women got radar, they find where you're weak."

"It must seem laughable to you, a man my age..."

The boy inclined toward him, looking impossibly wise. "You don't have to feel embarrassed about it. You can talk to me."

This was the moment David had been waiting for, and also dreading. He looked into the boy's eyes, oddly pale in the fluorescent light, then lowered his gaze to this own hands, which he folded, hoping to hide a tremor. "All right, but it's the synagogue I want to talk about, what happened that day."

A silence as of stone walls.

"You and your brother committed a crime—a crime against people you don't even know. How long can we go on making chitchat as if nothing has happened?"

Rashid shrank down in his seat. "It wasn't my idea."

"I didn't think so, and yet you went along with it."

"How else to let people know we exist? A beer bottle, a strip of rag, a bit of petrol, and *bam!* Suddenly we've got everyone's attention—the reporters, the *pol's, Les Guignols de l'Info...*"

"But why target a place of worship?"

"I told you," the boy pleaded, "it wasn't my idea."

"Why not a government building or a weapons factory?"

"We weren't out to get ourselves killed. We're not suicide bombers. There wasn't enough petrol in those bombs to mow a lawn."

The air had grown too heavy to breathe. David felt his lungs fill with fire. "Someone could have been killed—did you stop to think about that?"

"My brother warned me it would go down like this. What do you want, anyway? You come here acting like my friend, like maybe you actually care." The boy's voice thinned to a whimper. "You're just one more *mufti*, worming your way into my brain."

"I'm just trying to understand."

Again the room went silent except for the sound of a guard tramping to the threshold to drone, "*Plus que cinq minutes.*"

Rashid bolted to his slippered feet and strode slouch-shouldered to the door. "We're done," he said, spreading his arms and legs for a pat-down.

"Hey!" David called. "Done, says who? *I'm* not done."

"You want to understand? Talk to my *educateur*. He's got all the dirt, all the theories, and guess what? He doesn't know shit and neither do you."

The guard stopped and crossed his beefy arms. "*Trois minutes.*"

Rashid lingered on the threshold.

"All right, so I'm not your fairy godfather, not Superman, but I do care. Why else am I here?"

The prisoner pulled himself up with wounded dignity.

"That's for you to figure out, David."

The sound of his own name, spoken not with anger but tenderness, brought David to the brink of tears. He nodded and turned quickly away. The corridor, dark and airless, seemed to stretch on forever. Rationing breath he stepped through a swinging door only to find himself in another corridor, darker than the first.

"Join me for coffee?" Lebrun, blocking his escape route like a portable landslide.

"I should get home." To tea and seedlings and the girlfriend who would rather sift abstractions than bear his child.

"*Pardon,* but you look like you've been through the wringer. Kid giving you heartache?"

Something in the lieutenant's tone—a smidgeon of humanity?—made David pause long enough for Lebrun to link an arm though his and tug in the direction of a glassed-in office. "You think because I wear this uniform that I'm tough and don't feel for these kids? You think I don't question the system or wrestle with doubt, but you're wrong. I'm Jewish myself." He nudged David into a straight-backed chair, strode briskly to an urn, and filled two Styrofoam cups with black coffee. "Lucky for me, my family immigrated from a shtetl in Belarus and I grew up French. How about you?"

"My family history is a tad hazy."

"Look, I've got nothing against Rashid, but I love this country and I'll roll cigars in Hades before I let a bunch of ungrateful foreigners who can't even be bothered to learn the language destroy our patrimony. A man defends what he loves."

"Rashid, too, is trying in his way to be a man."

"And I'm here to show him how."

They applied themselves to the coffee, dark and thick as

tar.

"Has there been any progress?" David ventured.

"The kid's a real brain, likes school, does his assignments, and keeps to himself. The social worker has recommended he be sent to a *centre de placement immediat*, a sort of halfway house. Problem is space—there isn't any—and sending him home would amount to a death sentence."

"How about the brother?"

"Emile? He'll be out soon and has already petitioned to have Rashid released to his charge."

"Would that be wise?"

Lebrun shrugged. "There are no good choices. The brother, at least, is a blood relation."

David finished his coffee, a penance, and sat torpid in the iron chair in the glass room, feeling the weight of the world press in on them. "Why this enmity between Arab and Jew? We're just one more minority."

"The longer I live, the more convinced I become that there's no way to be a Jew in this world and not be reviled. American Jews lobby and fundraise and use their political muscle to shape a society in which minorities can feel safe—and? They reinforce the very stereotypes they are trying to arrest. European Jews, who have plenty more to bitch about, are model citizens—patriotic, undemanding—and? No one notices. The gentiles of Europe, not all but most, don't give a damn that they've left their Jewish neighbors parentless, traumatized, lacerated. There are two histories of the Second World War on this continent: a) The Holocaust never happened, or b) If it happened, it was, in any case, nothing unique." Relentless as a rapper, he took an audible gulp of air. "And then there are the Israelis, the upstart Jews who dare to claim something as their own, who defend it. They are the most hated Jews of the lot, those hummus-breathing Uzi-toting monsters who will be the end of us all!"

"And?"

Lebrun popped his cheeks in exasperation.

"So what does one do?"

"*Rien.*"

"What do you mean nothing?"

"Just be human." The lieutenant, his bluster spent, upturned his chafed palms. "Be human and hope people will be more kind than unkind."

ROWENA'S DARK TWIN

Rowena had always been a sound sleeper but began suddenly to suffer insomnia. For hours she would lie awake beside David, holding in her imagination a reproduction of the era in which Charlotte Corday lived and the Reign of Terror that brought her short life to an end. She heard the rasping wheels of the tumbrils as they carried the condemned to the guillotine; saw the crowds of *sans-culottes* rage through the streets, hungry for bread and blood. Forty thousand heads lopped off like cabbages. The bravery! The butchery!

"Bad dream?" David murmured.

"Go back to sleep." She rose, pulled on a kimono, and padded across the hallway to her office.

It seemed natural to seek Corday at night. Her dark twin, viewed by moonlight, seemed not an enigma at all but so real she might have been a fourth resident of the *Vie Dorée*.

David, bare-chested, leaned in the office doorway.

Cornered, she filled her hands with papers and pretended to sort them. "Darned cicadas will drive me crazy."

"When did we last watch the sunrise together?" He swept past her, opened the shutters, and stood looking out. The sun and moon were both visible, and the dawn stretched between them like an unfurled hammock. David held out an arm. "Come, you'll miss it."

"Aren't you going to ask me how my book is coming along?" David, his expression placid, hardly an expression at all, continued to look out. She approached only far enough to bathe her bare feet in a puddle of sunlight. "Why do I get the feeling you're less than enthused by my subject?"

"I support your writing, you know that."

"No evasions."

"Very well, then." He turned his earnestness on her, a weapon more potent than cunning or wit. "It spooks me, your fascination with her—with whatever it is she represents. I can't grasp it. Her story suggests nothing to me but futility."

"Look at her in the context of her times: a poor woman from the provinces, a woman at a time when women were utterly without power, a woman who acted—boldly, independently, from the heart."

"From the heart?" He repeated the words haltingly, as if the language were suddenly foreign to him. "She killed a man."

"To save a way of life."

David exhaled into a cupped hand.

"Out with it."

"Do I know you, Rowena?"

She looked past him to where the fields worked their geometry, suggesting order and abundance. Swijdendorp would be out with his mutts by then, casting about for his miraculous fungi. "I might ask the same of you. I don't know where you are half the time. You leave me in this house with your crazy mother—"

"Mum's not crazy."

"Of course not, she just thinks she's the Queen of England. I suppose that makes you the Prince of Wales."

He winced and went a shade paler. "Okay, so I've been

spending time away. There are things a man must do sometimes. Private things."

"Private? I crossed an ocean to share your life, your bed, and you can't confide in me?"

They squinted at each other in the unsparing light of morning. She felt sorry for him, for the fear he had this once let her see and the desire he had never been able to hide.

MOVING MYSTERIOUSLY

David returned to the prison next visiting day and waited for Rashid in the airless cubicle with its iron table and chairs. A security camera tracked him like a third eye. Not wanting to appear self-conscious, he set down his bag of baklava, drew in his elbows, and fixed his gaze on the blank wall.

At last Rashid, bone and sinew within his baggy clothes, entered and took a seat across from him. "I didn't think you'd come back, after... not that I'm apologizing."

"Neither am I."

They sat cross-armed and silent for what seemed a long time.

"You had a right to ask those questions," Rashid said at last.

"A right? I don't know about things like that, I just want to make sense of this, of us—am I a fool to think that we might have something to learn from each other?"

"If you're a fool, then so am I."

David breathed deeply for the first time. "Is there anything you need?

"Good one, mister. As if you could wave a magic wand."

"Okay, maybe I am just asking for form. There may not be a lot I can do for you right now, but damn it, can't you just once give me the benefit of the doubt?"

"You try living in this place. Like I told you before, don't expect sympathy."

David sank back into his seat and rubbed his temples, which had begun to throb. "You once asked me why I visit you. I've thought about it. Something tainted and false began to seep into my life when I was about your age; perhaps, in trying to become a man, I let go of something I oughtn't— my roots, my dreams… It's hard to explain."

Rashid, looking impossibly wise, recited from Lawrence, "*The old dreams are beautiful, beloved, soft-toned and sure, but the dream-stuff is molten and moving mysteriously…*"

"*Alluring my eyes, for I, am I not also dream-stuff?*"

The boy inclined toward him like a biblical prophet come to lead him out from the desert. "I get it, mister. I get it."

Somehow David knew that he would.

BEST OF THE CROP

At four p.m. Madame Fermat tramped through the chateau opening shutters. The west-facing rooms filled with light and birdsong, the east with intimation. Rowena wandered from one side to the other, unsettled by the brilliance and equally ill at ease in the shadows. The afternoon heat hung trapped within the corridors, which afforded no view out, only a monochrome imitation of twilight.

Weary of tapping out platitudes only to delete them a moment later, Rowena switched off her laptop. By following the clack-clack of Madame Fermat's clogs she plotted an escape route. A side door was best, out of view of both the garden and Miriam's bedroom window. Stealth, though not necessary, imbued these outings with an excitement they otherwise lacked. She had no destination (at least this was what she told herself), but more often than not she would find herself at Swijdendorp's rough-hewn gate, listening to the wheezing bark of his barrel-necked truffle dogs. This particular afternoon, she stumbled upon the farmer himself, roadside, pounding in fence posts with an enormous sledgehammer.

"I could use a hand," he said, straightening the post. "If you would just hold this upright…" He took a nail from his pocket and clamped it between his teeth. "Hold on."

She felt his hammer bear down. "I thought for a moment you might be genuinely glad to see me."

"I am," he assured her, rearing back for another blow.

"How many more of these do you have to set?"

He made a choppy motion with his crumpled work glove. "Five or six hundred, I reckon."

"Heck, I quit."

"Little hard work never hurt anyone, woman."

"Not what I had in mind," she said, gazing down the dirt track that led to the river.

"Wait, I have something for you at the house. Come with me."

She turned and studied the Dutchman in profile, his features slack from the morning's exertions, filmy with sweat. He had begun to walk toward the gate—he walked the same way he did everything else, without a single unnecessary movement. At the gate he broke pace, strode ahead to a squat outbuilding, and returned with a small burlap sack at the bottom of which clustered a dozen ripe plums. "Best of the crop."

When she hesitated to take them, he thrust the sack into her hands and began to walk toward the three-sided workshop. "So, how are things at the castle?" he asked.

"Can't complain."

"You're spoiled. Worst thing for a writer."

At the threshold she slung down her load and looked around. Every surface stood heaped with projects—farm equipment undergoing repair, a half-completed oak hutch, a dozen latticework trellises… There seemed no end to the Dutchman's industry, no rest for his able hands.

"You have a great deal to learn from the French," he went on. "You are too doctrinaire, too rigid, there's no play in you; and yet, you're a man's mistress. There's a glow about you he can't fully keep for himself. Your skin, here—" He ran the back of his roughened fingers along her collarbone.

"Stop it, Arjen."

"See, you're a puritan. How inconvenient." He took a fine-toothed saw down from its peg. "I had hoped to have an affair with you."

She stepped back, needing to lean against something. "You're forgetting about David."

"Not for a moment. But he's the wrong man, you know."

"We're still getting to know each other."

He sank the saw's honed teeth into a length of two-by-four. "You know him already, but he'll never know you."

"I prefer it that way. And as for you—"

"Spare yourself the bother: I'm presumptuous, arrogant, crude, a libertine, a vulture… My wife spelled it all out quite clearly."

"You have a wife?"

"*Had*. She threw herself into a river."

"How terrible!"

"I was joking." Arjen laughed, a sound barely distinguishable from the rasp of his saw.

"You're everything she said you were."

He went on sawing. "One day you'll beg me to make love to you."

Rowena veered and stormed out of the workshop, leaving behind the burlap sack. Arjen's truffle dogs, tied to a nearby tree, began in unison to yip. The midday sun pinned her shadow to the dry earth, and the only way home was upon the blackened ribs of her own reflection.

DAVID'S EDEN

The garden steadily wasted. Clinging to a wan vestige of fecundity, David got the gardener Durand's number and arranged a consultation for the following day. The old man puttered up the driveway in a pre-war Citroen, tossed a cigarette butt from the open window, and bounced out, managing somehow to look shorter standing than seated. He wore a hunting cap. They shook hands and gradually made their way about the grounds, pausing before each stem and stump.

Their first stop was a venerable old fig tree, its branches drooping like a worn mop. Monsieur Durand ran a thumbnail along the bark, squatted on his haunches to paw at the soil around the roots, then sniffed both hands. Taking the cap from his head, clutching it to his heart with a doleful expression, he pronounced, "*Mort.*"

They proceeded to the next tree, a balding apricot planted only weeks before. Monsieur Durand plucked a leaf and rolled it between his fingers. Nose to the ground, he crawled about the roots on all fours. Again his cap descended: "*Mort.*"

David led the gardener to a third tree, a mere sapling. Durand dropped to his knees. The Englishman could see Durand's nostrils quiver as he scooped up handfuls of soil and mournfully sifted them. He reached for his cap.

"*Mort,*" David preempted him.

"*Mort,*" echoed Monsieur Durand. "Too much

fertilizer."

David hired the old gardener, and the next day he showed up at seven a.m. wearing gumboots and dragging a pickaxe. He talked to himself as he worked, or perhaps he only grumbled. At ten a.m. sharp he sat with his back against the shed and drank the contents of a thermos bottle.

Feeling idle and hoping to reconnect with the fresh green tingle of weeks past, David donned his straw gardening hat and walked out to join him. "Mind if I give you a hand?"

Monsieur Durand lumbered to his feet. "*Comme vous voulez*," he said with thinly veiled disdain and trudged ahead.

David followed, mesmerized by the rhythmic squeak of the gardener's rubber boots. "Are you able to salvage anything?"

The Frenchman clicked a thumbnail against his front teeth. "Do the dead rise from the grave?"

David asked no more questions, contented himself with the mindless chores Durand deemed fit to delegate. With the air blowing featherlike across his face, he dug and hoed and moved earth. At the sight of each open bud he felt himself inflate with prospect. He planted a pair of date palms at the hill's crest—new life for old, new life for a man at his prime's far edge. He had only to grab hold.

LIONEL GOES APE

The *Fête National* divides each summer in half: the tube of tanning oil already tacky, vacations begun, traffic gridlocked. It is a day Lionel always approaches with trepidation, knowing full well that whatever festivities he plans and however he goes about realizing them, the result will not please. Old-timers will want more accordion music, more pageantry, enough goose liver to dam a river; the younger set jazz and amusement park rides. No matter how much he spends on fireworks, someone will hark back to a bigger, more impressive display. Even before Lionel could pry himself from bed, a mild, if relentless, dread hounded him.

He performed his morning toilette with particular care and padded downstairs, dressed except for his feet, which remained defiantly bare.

"Benoit called," Laura informed him, pouring a first cup of coffee (by day's end, he will have dosed himself with a dozen). "Something about the audio system."

"Don't tell me it's acting up again. Every year…"

"At least he's consistent."

Bracing for a day of shirtsleeves diplomacy, he gulped a last sip of coffee, stepped into his moccasins, and donned his cap.

"*A bientôt, Capitaine.*"

Laura, her bosom full and inviting against his ribs, kissed him with more than the usual application. He had to force himself out the door. His air of purpose inflated as he rounded the corner and entered the village's compact hub. There was the usual tangle of traffic, vacationers moving on to the next wine tasting, the next signposted scrap of history. Too early for most pedestrians, Russ Griffith streaked by in his negligible nylon shorts. Lionel, doffing his cap on reflex, crossed to the opposite pavement.

Benoit's workshop, tucked behind the boules court, emitted an earsplitting cackle of static. As Lionel approached, the double doors swung open and a pair of massive amplifiers rolled forward, obscuring a crouched Benoit, who even at that early hour wore the sweat-soaked brow of the technologically thwarted. "*C'est chouette, hein?*" he intoned, rising for a handshake. "They'll hear us on the Champs-Elysee."

"They'll hear us on Pluto."

Lionel continued on to the *mairie,* which draped in the blue, red and white of the Republic provided a focal point for the day's festivities. The hired folding chairs had arrived. Moving with the hunched grace of a bull, the street cleaner arranged them in concentric rows about a makeshift bandstand, gradually filling the square.

This year's celebration was to feature two costumed apes dancing the Macarena, a face-painting booth, old man Gaultier's trio (accordion, bagpipes and hurdy-gurdy) followed by the ubiquitous Benoit, doubling as DJ, and finally, just past sunset, the mandatory fireworks display guaranteed to disappoint. By design the celebration has little to do with the storming of the Bastille. The citizens of Beautemps have always taken pride in their distance from Paris, a distance both geographic and temperamental. That their village forms part of a great nation, who would debate? That the French Revolution forged the foundations of free society, any school child knows. But on this day in high summer it is themselves they celebrate, they whose ancestral ties to the land predate Joan of Arc. They who have stayed rooted *malgré tout.*

Gaultier, coolly appraising, stood off to one side of the square. Though the sun was already overhead he wore his signature woolen beret and silk cravat. Strapping on his pipes, he nodded in Lionel's direction, adjusted the tilt of his hat, and continued his inspection.

Lionel entered the *mairie* and found Leclerc inflating balloons with a bicycle pump. They shook hands, sending the cumulus multi-colored mass gently bobbing. Beneath Leclerc's heel the pump gave a hiss. "Ape suits just arrived, bill's on your desk."

"Hope they're ventilated."

Leclerc shook his ponderous head.

The mayor reached on reflex for his collar button, but

it was already open. "If you need me, I'll be in my office."

The festivities were scheduled to begin at two, and still the sound system belched deafening blasts of static. He watched from his office window as Benoit wrestled the speakers into place, then the microphone. The ape suits lay draped across an armchair. He tore away their plastic wrappings.

"Brilliant! Which one is mine?" He turned to find David Crown gamboling across the threshold. The Englishman extended his right hand for a shake and with the other petted the costumes' faux fur. "I brought the CD player," he said and switched it on.

Lionel took a few dance steps, switched it off, and dropped into a chair. Already he could feel the first beads of sweat dampen his collar.

"We really must rehearse," David insisted. "Frankly, I'm not much of a dancer."

"I need a cup of coffee—how about you?"

"Come now, let's put the costumes on, shall we? It's been awhile since I was an ape and I wouldn't want to appear excessively evolved." Before Lionel could protest, David picked up the shaggier of the suits and began to wriggle into it. Resigned, he did the same.

"*Bof,* I'm suffocating."

"Nothing to be done about it." Again David flicked on the music and began at once to move to it.

"*Ça groove! C'est mortel!*" The mayor doubled over his desk, laughing until his ribs chafed. David danced on in perfect rhythm, his hands moving crisscrossed from shoulders to hips and back again, his furry derriere working.

"Hi ho, we need to syncopate—or do I mean synchronize?"

"No matter, my friend. *Tu es une vraie bombe!*"

"Is that good or bad?"

"Turn up the volume," Lionel shouted through the costume's one air hole. "I can't hear inside this rug."

"What did you say? Headgear's heavy as a muffler."

Lionel sucked in air. Planting himself beside David, he aped the Englishman's movements, straining to keep pace.

"Bit like drill team."

"*Aie,* it's like a furnace in here!"

"May I suggest a tad more hip action?"

To Lionel's relief the song ended in a low sigh of static. Panting, he struggled out of his rubberized hood and wrung out the collar of his *Lacoste*. "Ready for that coffee now?"

Without warning the music started in again, the Beatles yelping in their indecipherable Liverpudlian, "*Sheik it oop, bebe now!* " Without missing a beat David burst into an exuberant *au go-go*. "How's this for an encore?" he shouted above the din, dancing, grinding, beating his chest, an entirely convincing ape, and yet somehow also entirely himself.

David's Dose of Reality

David took a last sip of Earl Grey then circled the kitchen table to where his mother sat, absently leafing through the morning's junk mail—a sale circular from Monsieur Bricolage, a postcard announcing a change in recycling procedures, the latest gossip from a local psychic calling herself Madame Cosmique…

"I fancy some nice smoked salmon, the kind we used to get on the East End. What was it called, that place with the pickle barrels outside?"

"Before my time, Mum."

"It was the best of times, it was the worst of times—did I just make that up?"

"Dickens may have beat you to it." He kissed her

withered cheek, wiped away a dab of strawberry jam. "I may not make it home for tea this afternoon. Errands to run."

It was visiting day. David instructed Madame Fermat to serve Miriam's lunch in the conservatory—the sunlight would do her good—and to make sure his mother's pills accompanied the tea tray.

"And *L'Americaine?*"

"Working. Best not to disturb her."

With breakfast over and the residents of the *Vie Dorée* shut away in their separate rooms, David opened a window and gazed out. Durand was already at work on the grounds, spreading a foul-smelling concoction at the base of his newly planted cypress trees. The only sound a muted, if persistent, ringing. Who would call at this hour with half the populace sleeping off hangovers and the other half pacing the curbs for the bread truck? David, already en route to the door with a volume of Neruda under his arm, didn't stop to answer the phone, leaving Madame Fermat no choice but to call from the upstairs landing in a voice that might have brought down the walls of Jericho, "*Monsieur Lebrun vous demande!*"

David retraced his steps as far as the library, closed the thick oak door behind him, and picked up the receiver.

"We've got a problem," the lieutenant said without preamble. "Rashid has assaulted a guard—the runt can really throw a punch, it turns out. *Mec* lost a tooth."

"I'm on my way."

"Not until the kid chills. There's a protocol for these cases."

"But what happened? Rashid wouldn't just launch into someone unprovoked."

"Immaterial. He knew the rules."

Not for the first time David felt himself utterly helpless. "What next?"

"Another few weeks and he would have walked out of

here free as a bird, but now… "They sabotage themselves, these kids. They go ballistic. *Merde.* Call me in a few days and I'll see what I can finagle."

"Can you get a message to him?"

"Shoot."

"Tell him, 'Light breaks where no sun shines, where no sea runs.' Tell him to look in Thomas."

"A poem?" The lieutenant's cynicism seeped through the headset like acid. "You think you can save these kids with pretty words? *Tu délires!* What you need, Crown, is a dose of reality. *Merde.*"

David, having come to feel a grudging respect for Lebrun, fought the urge to take a jab of his own. "I'll call in a few days. I'll be there."

FRESH START

Tired of waiting for the telephone to ring, David took to puttering in the garden on the heels of the crusty Durand. The gardener tolerated his presence but did not deign to make conversation. If either unwittingly uttered a word, it was to the shoots and buds.

The roar of an unmuffled engine made David look up. Lebrun dismounted from his Triumph with the contained grace of a toreador. "Crown!" he called, striding toward him with the beneficent aggression the Englishman had come to expect.

The lieutenant took him by the arm and tugged toward shade. "What a sour mug on that old codger," he remarked, pointing with his unshaven chin toward the gardener, who as if oblivious of their presence, continued to work.

"Durand? He's all right." David pulled off his gardening gloves and set them down on a statue of Leila and the Swan. "I phoned your office."

"There are matters best spoken of in person."

Something in the lieutenant's mien, a forced nonchalance, augured the worst. "Bad news?"

"*Pas du tout*. Rashid's situation has been resolved in record time."

"Then I can see him?"

"He's gone. To Lyon, a quieter facility."

"Just like that?"

"Nothing is ever *just like that*. The kid has an uncle there, the kind that still holds a job and doesn't make trouble. Nothing but trouble around here."

"It's hardly a solution."

"You got a solution, I'm sure President Chirac would love to hear it. The kid's off my turf. *Fini*. I wish him well." Lebrun, his signature swagger absent, began to walk away. "Who do you think I am, God almighty?" As if summoned, he stopped dead and fished a crumpled letter out of his hip pocket. "From Rashid. Write to him if you want. I jotted down the mailing address on the envelope."

David took the letter, and waiting for Lebrun to go, turned it over in his hands.

"I know you wanted better for the kid," said the lieutenant. "If it's any consolation, so did I."

"I guess this is goodbye then."

"You never know. The way the world's going… but Crown, I was rooting for you."

"You talk as if it's over. The boy hasn't even turned sixteen."

Lebrun sadly shook his head and started back down the hill. "If I can be of service, you know where to find me."

David watched him mount his bike, kick the starter, and tear off down the driveway.

As he turned back toward the grounds his gaze locked with Durand's, a scant second, but long enough to chill the air between them. David wondered, not for the first time, what gripe the old gardener might be nursing.

"Durand, are you happy working here?"

"Where else would I work?"

"Right."

In silence they returned to their separate patches of earth and resumed their gardening.

DISAPPEARED

Cher David,

I would have said goodbye, but these *keufs* want me out of their hair and a van is already waiting outside to make me disappear. If you don't hear from me again, they've probably shot me and dumped my body in a ditch somewhere—that was a joke, mister.

They're sticking me in a pen on the outskirts of Lyon; a fresh start, they call it. I've got to hand it to Lebrun, that *mec* will do anything to protect his mates. *Raton* one of them nicknamed me, like the rodent. Called my mother a used-up whore no Frenchman would have married. They all said things. But there was one, the one who reported me, who was always staring at my butt as I walked by. He would look at it and whistle, like I was a homo. It never failed to get a laugh.

Like I told you, they won't let me live and won't let me die.

I've got to go. The men in white suits have come for me. Father Justice is baring his fangs. You were right about a few things, if that makes you feel any better. Anyway, you had the poems.

Je t'embrasse,

Rashid

A DREAM DEFERRED

Rashid:

Thank you for your letter (the contents of which I will tackle further on). Lebrun gave me your address.

How are you? How do you like your new digs (I can almost see the *get-real-mister* look on your face)? For the record, I had no say in the matter and can only hope that the authorities have acted in your best interests.

Lebrun tells me, if you stay out of trouble, you may be released within the month. Until you are once again a free man, you have two choices—and you're not going to like either one. Either you a) steel your nerves and choose not to react to the baiting and provocation or b) resort to violence and give your jailers a reason to keep you incarcerated.

Please write and let me know how you get on. And do think about your future and what sort of mark you'd care to leave on this less-than-perfect world. Inaction is a crime against oneself. Langston Hughes knew this better than either of us when he wrote, *"What happens to a dream deferred? Does it dry up like a raisin in the sun?"*

David

CHIMERAS

It wasn't long before Lionel and David were again called into action. Swijdendorp's poachers had struck a second time.

The farmer, hell-bent on protecting his precious fungi, took to patrolling his fields well into the night. Sleep deprivation took a toll on the *Hollandais*. His speech grew thick, he neglected to cut his hair (or to wash it for that matter), and his lower lip drooped like a fish ready for the pan. His predicament outraged the few neighbors in whom he chose to confide. Armed with hunting rifles, they joined in his vigil. Having circled the property for three hours without encountering any predator larger than a muskrat, however, they tired of the manhunt and began to head for home. Only Lionel and David refused to abandon the search. The night turned blustery, ablaze with stars. They were alone with the nocturnal creatures, shadows like themselves.

"This is freedom!" the Englishman rhapsodized in a whisper.

For Lionel land could never be other than travail. He had seen his father labor in the fields through good seasons and bad, his back gradually bending and a look of perpetual supplication etching itself on his brow. There were gods to appease, politicians to court, pests to foil… a thousand and one cares repeated, multiplied, in a never-ending cycle.

"Between land and sea there can be only one choice."

David's flashlight skimmed along a row of oaks.

In the end it was not the family farm that lowered Lionel's sails but the will of a tender-lipped woman, who longed for a home and would not compromise. "A beautiful girl doesn't wait forever."

"Nor should she. How *is* Laura?"

"Fired-up about a bunch of nonsense. Politics!" He drew an index finger along his hairline. "I've had it up to here."

"One feels so powerless."

"Lebrun told me about Rashid. Perhaps it's for the best. He gets a second chance, and you? Isn't it time you stop worrying about a screwed-up little tough and start living the *vie dorée?*"

"Rashid is not who you imagine. Confused, yes, but bright, funny, sensitive, a lover of poetry…"

"You sound like a doting father. This boy is nothing to you. He meant you harm—or have you forgotten?"

"There's a bond. I can't explain it."

"David, David… you have family, a girlfriend, a beautiful home, and the leisure to savor it all. If I were you, I would fish and drink rivers of wine. Make love. *Vive la vie!*"

They sipped coffee from a thermos, wove through a half-picked patch of ripe parsnips.

"What do you know about Durand?"

"The old-timer has lived in Beautemps all his life except for the wars, when he did his military duty. He was widowed a few years ago. His one daughter, mousey little thing, went off to do missionary work somewhere. Why do you ask?"

"I can't make him out. There's something almost hostile about him. He's angered by the oddest things—even Lebrun noticed."

"Lebrun could write a book on antisocial behavior."

"He has succeeded in driving me out of my own garden."

"No crime in that." Lionel hooked an arm through David's, the better to steer through the maze of vegetables. "There's nothing else for him, *mon ami*—no work, no *famille*. Every day there are more like him, marginalized old people left to fend for themselves. He needs that job."

"The job is his. I just wish he would smile once in a while."

"*Bof*, enjoy your begonias and let the old geezer be."

They walked on. Less inclined to speak as the hour grew late, they followed their torch beams up and down the ebony fields. At the property's far edge a jot of light danced across a tree trunk and swiftly vanished. David began to sprint toward it, faster on his feet than Lionel would have expected of a man who had spent his life at a desk.

"Kill your flashlight," Lionel said, running alongside David with his eyes scouring the distance.

There was nothing to be seen and yet they raced on, buffeted by the wind, stung by purpose—the Swijdendorps of the world must not stand alone! If the poacher dared to show his face, he would have a fight on his hands. This was no Jean Valjean quelling his family's hunger with a pilfered loaf of bread but a human parasite indulging a corrupted palate.

"We've lost him," David sighed.

The distant light flickered once again, spurring them on. By this time, Lionel's heart was hammering and each breath cost him; David took the lead, propelling himself forward with audible huffs. The fields sprawled before them, mined with hazards: nettles, exposed roots, the odd stake. They stumbled and righted themselves only to stumble again.

"The cagey so-and-so keeps changing direction."

"*Bof*, it's like chasing a chimera."

"Look, over there!" Altering course, the Englishman began to race toward a moving shadow of indistinct dimensions, a shadow that might have been boar or man, or neither.

Lionel followed, regretting having refused Swijdendorp's rifle. The poacher might well have been armed. Slowing pace, he dipped at the knee to pocket a stone.

"It's gone," David's voice drifted back.

And then the barking began, or perhaps it had been there all along, drowned out by the fanfare inside their heads. Before they could take cover, the truffle dogs, a pair of them, were darting toward them, howling as they came. Lionel heaved the stone at the nearer of the two, and it yipped and fell back.

"Crikey," David groaned as the other sunk its teeth into his leg.

Lionel started forward but a beam of light blinded him.

"*Arrêtez!*" called the unseen stalker. "Stop or I'll shoot!"

Gathering his wits, Lionel switched on the flashlight. "Swijdendorp, you *charlot*, call off your dogs. Bloodthirsty little monsters."

The *Hollandais* collared the more insistent of his curs and shuffled backwards with a sheepish shrug. "They're only doing their job."

"Are you all right, David?"

"Never been better," the Englishman replied, briefly examining the torn hem of his trousers. He stood upright, craned his neck. "Have you ever seen so many stars?"

Lionel looked up in spite of himself. The sky swelled with light, bled light, the planets had caught fire.

The farmer yawned. "I'd better head home. Pole beans to harvest tomorrow…"

Lionel heard him shoulder the rifle and trudge off with his dogs softly panting.

THE BOOK OF GRAY

Cher Habibi,

You don't give up, do you? I thought you would be relieved to have me gone, the same as Lebrun, but here's your letter (nice penmanship, by the way).

I've been in this dive a week and haven't thumped anyone—which isn't to say I haven't wanted to. Why are these places so full of assholes? The one person who's cool (and hot) is my *educateur*, Sonia. If you didn't already have a girlfriend, I would hook you two up.

My brother will be freed next week and heading to Lyon to look for work. Prospects aren't great, but the sooner he lands a job and can rent a flat, the sooner I'll be out of this bunker.

I know, I know, I'm supposed to be thinking about the future, but my mind won't go there. So many walls in this place, walls everywhere I turn. Maybe it will be easier on the outside, where a *mec* can look up at the sky or zone out on the tram.

It's the past I think about. Like, could I have not been such a screw-up? Maybe if I had known someone like you before all this happened, but who pays attention to *mecs* like me until we screw up? How would you and I have met? Where? Your world ends where mine begins.

I'm not making excuses for what I did. You haven't asked for an apology, and I'm not about to make one. When anger is eating at your gut every minute, when you're so angry you can't tell black from white, you've got to let rip. Why a synagogue? Because it was there. My brother says it's the Jews who keep us down. Everyone says so. I couldn't tell you this to your face, David, but I needed to hate someone, and it was easiest to hate the same people my friends hated.

Sonia is into D.H. Lawrence big time, did I tell you?

"And so I sit and scan the book of gray
Feeling the shadows like a blind man reading
All fearful lest I find the last words bleeding
With wounds of sunset and the dying day."

Votre ami dévoué,
Rashid

SERMON

Rashid:

Thank you for your latest, which was most enlightening. I'm grateful for your candor, truly I am, even when what is revealed causes me worry or pain. The past, though not forgotten, fades over time and a man can choose a different path. I would like to think you have made that choice, even if the way forward is not clear from where you stand.

As for your remark about Jews, it is a lie, the sort of lie out of which tragedies are made. While you believe such things, how can I be sure of your friendship? When next you feel rage well up inside you, will I be the target of it?

I would like to help you. But first, help yourself by questioning deep in your heart the rhetoric and stereotypes you have accepted as truth. Break free of them! Look at the world through fresh eyes and the future will open to you.

This may sound like a sermon, but it's what I know.

David

DAVID AT A CROSSROADS

With the garden beginning to provide a bit of privacy David splurged on a large outdoor tub, which with the help of a local excavator he sunk in a sheltered yet sunny spot beside the house. Mornings, before Madame Fermat arrived, he and Rowena would slip out to luxuriate in the tepid currents. It was the oasis he had hoped for: songbirds in their fullest throat, sun at its mildest, and butterflies of blue and gold bursting from the foliage like confetti.

One morning they lingered longer than usual, weightlessly spooning. How little David desired beyond that tub; he wanted only to prolong the moment. An impossibility. Madame Fermat was never late.

He pressed his lips to Rowena's neck, and she gave an odd little squeal.

"Excitable, aren't you?"

Rowena dipped down, submerging her breasts. "Who the hell is that?" she uttered, pointing with her glance.

David's brother Barry, dressed for business, stood a few paces away. "Good morning, Davey," he said with the overblown affability usually reserved for large accounts. "And you must be?"

"David's concubine." Rowena's smile held a shameless glee.

"Hardly," David countered, hoping to impose decorum. "Rowena and I met in the States. Mother must have told you."

"Of course, the commoner of suspect origins."

"Is that what she calls me? Why doesn't she doesn't just say Polack, like everyone else?"

Barry laughed, a sure sign of nervousness. Laughter was foreign to his nature. It looked wrong on his face, a smear of egg, a pox.

"But what brings you here?"

"I was just passing through. New parent company has its eye on France, the greedy bastards. Can't say I mind the scenery." He made a show of looking over the grounds. "So, this is the decaying splendor you were so keen for... has a certain charm, I must admit."

"Would you mind?" David motioned toward their robes, which lay on a nearby chaise.

"Sorry," Barry said, turning his back. "I took you for naturists."

They wrapped hurriedly. Rowena excused herself, promising to join them for breakfast.

"I didn't realize she was so..." Barry stole a last glance as she made her way through the conservatory, drying her gleaming skein of hair. "*Gawd,* she looks a teenager. You look quite the lad yourself." David's brother, despite his designer coif and whitened teeth, looked his sixty years. He had the yellowed undertones of the perpetually fatigued, and his hairline had receded farther than David's own.

"Joanne and the girls well?"

Pivoting, Barry continued his inspection. "I was expecting something a bit more..."

"Rustic? Consider it a work in progress. I'm still

fiddling with the details."

"Didn't know you could swing a hammer. Manual dexterity was never your strong suit."

"Don't start in again about the adding machine roll."

David braced for the usual dressing-down, but instead Barry said. "If you think I'm envious, you're right. What man wouldn't be?" He gave his brother what was no doubt intended as a wink, a contraction of the eye muscles, in any case.

"How long are you here for?"

"Cup of tea. Papers to sign up the road."

"I'd better get mother up."

"Later." Barry extricated himself from his sports jacket, daubed at his forehead with a monogrammed handkerchief. "How is she?"

"Not bad. The Aricept seems to have alleviated her symptoms. She can be stunningly lucid, sometimes."

"And the rest of the time?"

"We get by."

The perspiration was beginning to bead on Barry's forehead.

"Shall we go in?" David suggested, motioning his brother ahead. "Miriam will be delighted to see you. But tell me, what brings you?"

"Had a little scare with the old ticker."

"A heart attack?"

"Nothing major, but enough to jar a man to his senses. I'm backing off from the company—hell, it's not ours anyway. Why should I kill myself?"

"I was afraid you might one day."

"Dad did, but he had a reason to. He came up from nothing, it was work or starve. We've had it handed to us."

"Forced on us."

"You're complaining?" He gestured around him,

indicating the tapestries and paintings, the marble staircase and gilded mirrors. "Always the delicate one, yet you took like the rest."

"I worked. Willy Crown was no charity."

"But he was. Half the family sponged off him, or didn't you bother to notice? No, you were too busy whining, as if working for a living was just your tough luck."

"Let's drop it."

They crossed the foyer and entered the kitchen. Barry, too jowly for so early in the day, draped his jacket across a chair back. "Look, I haven't come to argue. I've come to— hell, I wish we could talk. Can't we just talk?"

"Try me."

"I'm sixty years old, I've got a bad heart, my family has made lives for themselves. Lives that don't include me."

"That could change."

"The kids are out on their own already and Joanne's always on the run with friends— volunteering, lunching, the garden club..."

"Sounds like you need a hobby."

"I need more than a hobby." He lowered his head and his chin hung in fleshy folds. "I miss Mum. I didn't think I would."

"Let me fetch her—"

"Not yet. There's something we need to settle. I'm nearly retired now; I rarely travel. I'd like to do my part for Miriam, back home. Surely she'd rather be in familiar surroundings, hearing her own language, near her grandchildren."

"What exactly are you proposing?"

"Come back to England—you're welcome to bring your American friend with you, of course. Look, I heard what happened to you here. You're better off back home. More respectable class of Arabs."

"Not *you* too." But his brother's tone was conciliatory; it augured a pact David could ill afford to rebuff. "I appreciate what you're saying, but I haven't given up on France. Far from it. I've never been happier."

"Happy today isn't necessarily happy tomorrow. Just think about it. In the meantime, send mother home for a holiday. Late September, say?" They shook on it. "Davey, I know we've had our differences…"

"Mum still gets on me about my general uselessness."

"I understand why you've gone your own way. It wasn't so bad early on. I took to the business like a shark to water, but it's no damn fun anymore. And I'm tired, bloody tired."

"All that's over. Your life is your own now."

"Some life."

David placed a hand on his brother's shoulder, the sunken knob that had borne the weight of an empire. "I'll send mother home," he assured Barry. "We'll work something out."

EVERY FRUIT IN SODOM

It was early August when Rowena lost Corday's trail. She read and reread the manuscript pages she had written, asking herself what she had hoped to prove. How many times can a writer exhume a corpse before it loses all likeness to itself, takes on the waxen freakishness of an effigy? Pitched into a vacuum, Rowena clung to routine. Mornings she would shut herself away in her office, switch on the computer, and sit numb-headed before the flashing cursor.

Jean-Marie Marat came to haunt her. Ugsome, he would rise up out of his bath like some imaginary sea monster, declaiming the Rights of Man. With each resurgence his knife wound would flap open, spouting blood, while beneath, wreathed in spume, his penis dangled like a dead sardine. Desperate to fill the computer screen, she took to copying excerpts from his autobiography. She tried to see Marat as Corday did—as destroyer, tyrant, a canker on society—but she couldn't. The stubborn fact of his humanity remained. She knew then that her novel was doomed.

The hours alone that she had guarded so fiercely began to cloy. Like David she was left without an occupation, but rather than seek his company, she avoided him. A matter of pride. She wasn't ready to admit defeat, not to him, who had had faith in her and bankrolled her failure.

By afternoon, already plotting escape, she would find herself listening for the passage of Madame Fermat's clogs. The housekeeper's movements had become as predictable to Rowena as the latching of a shutter. Miriam was harder to track. She had taken to prowling the halls at night, sleeping through breakfast, taking tea in the conservatory wearing nothing but a satin slip and tassel loafers. Miriam she avoided by scent; the old woman marked her trail with florid, woozy-making perfumes.

To slip out a rear door into the seductive heat of a summer day—the breeze on her skin, its luring whisper, made Rowena race. Her instinct was always to take cover, which meant running toward the tree-lined lane, beyond which lay the fields. Swijdendorp's still held towering green husks of sweet corn and boulder-sized orange squashes. As she passed his gate the farmer, digging nearby, glanced in her direction.

"You forgot your plums," he said gruffly, continuing to assault the ground with his shovel.

She approached as far as the fence.

He halted his thrusts long enough to observe, "You're getting too much sun." He took the pitiful canvas hat from his bowl of hair and held it out. "Here, put this on."

Disarmed by the gesture, she opened the gate and

walked through.

"We could use some rain," he said and began again to dig.

She gave the hat a brushing-off. "You don't change, do you?"

"Do I need to? You always come back."

"You happen to be in my path."

He paused his shovel and rested his hands atop its metal handle. "Still bored? Haven't you made any friends?"

"Friends? I've alienated everyone. Thanks to me, David barely has a social life anymore."

"David is agreeable; they will find it in their hearts to forgive him."

"He's too decent to blame me."

"Either that or gun-shy. Some men will do anything to avoid a woman's wrath." Slinging the shovel over a shoulder, the farmer bent to cup a handful of earth. "Has he asked about us?"

"Us, meaning you and I? Of course not."

"But he must know you visit me. I've seen his mother's nose pressed against the windowpane each time you slip out the back door."

She waved the remark away. "Don't be ridiculous."

"Whatever we do or don't do, it will be assumed we have savored every fruit in Sodom, so why not do just that? Women have told me my lovemaking far surpasses my conversation. Your satisfaction is guaranteed."

"I won't ask for references."

"You have lost your shame. You no longer pinken at my advances."

"Perhaps that's because I no longer take them seriously."

The shovel dropped to the ground. The farmer sprang forward, cupped her buttocks with both dusty hands, and flicked his tongue along the hollow of her ear. "That is your mistake."

She pulled away and felt his clasp loosen. There was no struggle, only a ginger disengagement of limbs. She took his floppy, faded hat from her head—it smelled of dogs and lemongrass. "I won't be back this time."

Too unsettled to return to the chateau, she continued along the perimeter of the fields into the woods and along a secluded trail. Jackrabbits bounded by. Rowena walked reflecting on her time in Beautemps, on the misguided notions that had drawn her across an ocean and the failure that would send her back.

By the time she realized she was not alone, Cecil Rhodes was planted in her path like a sand trap. "Off gallivanting? I had heard you keep office hours."

"Just taking a break."

"And your *paramour*?" Anglicized, the term sounded sordid, as Cecil, no doubt, intended it to. "Haven't seen you two together for some time—well, honeymoons don't last forever. Even at your age."

"I need to get back for tea."

"Of course, a nod to routine and tradition. Such a dutiful son, your Mr. Crown, such a proper specimen. Yet here you are. Could it be that you prefer Swijdendorp's brand of masculinity—the sinew, the sweat, that goaty undertone. There's no accounting."

"I don't find that funny." Rowena quashed the urge to slap the Englishman's ruddy face.

"Who's trying be droll?" Cecil took an odd little wobble, looking for a moment like a sideswiped bowling pin. "Mr. Crown and my wife were friends, you know, before you arrived on the scene. There's a history. He trusted her eye, her taste, of which you are now the beneficiary."

"David is very grateful for Hedy's help."

"Alas, it wasn't gratitude she wanted, poor dear." Cecil gazed with a sort of awe toward the *Vie Dorée*. "She had a thing for him, and then you showed up, the little librarian from the colonies. You, every middle-aged man's fantasy—until you open your mouth. You certainly know how to put the kibosh on things."

"I think you've said enough."

The Englishman, large-pored and glassy-eyed, drew himself up. "No invitation to tea for the naughty Mr. Rhodes?"

"Another time, Cecil, when you're—"

"Another time then," he said, and poking himself in the ear, put on a pair of goggle-lensed dark glasses. "Crown, a cuckold? Hedy, I'm sure, will be tickled. Woman scorned and all that."

"You couldn't be more wrong about this."

"Methinks the lady doth protest too much." Tipsily weaving he continued along the lane.

MALGRÉ TOUT

Habibi,

You might as well be speaking Swahili. Every delinquent in the *banlieues* was once a sucker waiting to be sent on a course. I know *mecs* with diplomas from the *grandes écoles* who are stocking shelves at Carrefour.

But fuck all that. I'm used to people telling me that black is white; even Sonia has started to.

What I can't stomach is you questioning my friendship, like I can't think for myself, like I can't be trusted. I thought you knew me. Just once, can't you stop trying to be wise and sensible and say something real?

Votre ami malgré tout,
Rashid

DAVID GETS REAL

Rashid:

If getting real means spewing raw emotion, I'm not conditioned that way. If it means being frank, perhaps I can accommodate you.

From our first encounter you have shaken my world, my thinking, and forced me to confront situations foreign to my milieu, situations that overwhelm me and bring my inadequacies to the fore. It would be easier on my psyche to label you an enemy and leave you to your fate, whatever that may be. I didn't plant the hatred in your heart; neither can I remove it.

No one is immune to anger, myself included. Okay, so I've had a few privileges in life, but I know what discrimination is. I went to a fancy school where the term "Yid" was forever whispered at my back—not that I'm drawing a comparison. Each man's burden is uniquely his own.

I didn't mean to pontificate, but being your elder, is it not my place to try to spare you life's worst blows? I don't have a son. I still hope to, one day. In some ways my future is no clearer than yours, I've just got less time left to get it right.

David

RENT

Crown,

Bet you wasn't expecting to hear from me again. I wouldn't be writing, but what's this about you and Rashid? Why are you making nice-nice with my little brother? I never did trust your *Père Noël* cover—what's your game anyway?

Look, I'll keep this short (it's not like we're friends or anything). I could use some quick cash. For rent.

The address is on the envelope.

Rashid doesn't know I'm writing to you, so keep your *bouche fermée.* I don't need any more *keufs* breathing down my back.

Emile Hamadi

LIFE CRISIS

Nearly dusk. Lionel, locked in silent dialogue with his stuffed barracuda, gazed out at the *Riviere Rieux*, which seeming to brood, lay deserted. He supposed he was having a life crisis—nest empty, midsection expanding, marriage cooling by degrees... "I'm too young to feel this old," he told the fish.

The fish's one eye appeared to dilate. *"You're just like everyone else."*

Lionel would have liked to disagree, to rage against conformity, but deep down he knew himself to be the most ordinary of men.

"Am I interrupting something?" David Crown stood in the doorway, shuffling his sandaled feet on a hemp mat.

"Chess?"

"Might we row for a bit if it's not too late? Unwind."

"*Comme tu veux*," said Lionel, quickly securing the cash box and padlocking the kiosk door. "Full moon tonight."

The *Bora-Bora* was already in the water, tied to a small pier. Lionel held the boat steady while David, clearly no sailor, clumsily boarded. "I'll do the rowing."

Lionel cast off. The current carried them to the middle of the river, which held an undulating reflection of the night sky. The Englishman rowed with uncustomary vim. "Something troubling you, my friend?"

David mulled his response overlong. "Not especially."

"What do you hear from your surrogate son?"

"Rashid? It's been a while since his last letter."

"I'll make inquiries, if you'd like."

"Please, if it's not a bother."

"Shouldn't take more than a couple phone calls." Calls he would have preferred not to make. "David, David… young people are easily distracted. Rashid has moved on. You did what you could."

David's breathing had grown labored. Lionel tried to relieve him of the oars, but his friend kept hold, rowed harder.

"Have you thought about having children of your own?"

"I hope to, but—it's complicated." David turned the boat around with surprising deftness and rowed toward shore. The moon had risen, painting the river the color of burnished copper.

"Rowena? It's none of my business, but are you sure she's the one?"

"It's a wonder she puts up with me. My ex-wife iced my last birthday cake with shaving cream."

"Forget I asked."

David rested his oars and looked up. They drifted in an uneasy silence broken by the river's monotonous cackle—who was it mocking?

"Can we ever be sure, Lionel?" A fallen leaf, the first of the season, blew into the bow. "How little we know, how little we'll ever know."

FREEDOM

Rashid,

It has been a while since I last heard from you. Is everything all right? If what my sources tell me is accurate, you are once again a free man. I hope you will find life on the outside a pleasant enough challenge. Please get in touch if there is ever anything I can do for you. No parting words, just this plagiarized verse from Lawrence:

"And so I cross into another world
Shyly and in homage linger for an invitation
From this unknown that I would trespass on."
David Crown

HOUSEGUEST

If time could be turned back, the clock reset, minutes, hours, days reclaimed, this was life at the *Vie Dorée* as Indian summer drifted in and poured forth its honeyed light. The chateau could still have used a few finishing touches, but David, beyond caring about such trifles, awoke feeling that he had been given a reprieve.

He resolved to take Lionel's advice—to drink rivers of wine, to make love, to live! Was this not France, after all? Was he not the most fortunate man ever to own a hill?

His elation could not be contained. Bounding from bed like the sprinter he had once dreamed of becoming, racing barefoot along the corridor, he went in search of Rowena. She was not in her office. Crestfallen beyond all proportion, he continued his trajectory, opening and closing doors to rooms he seldom entered and barely recognized. He scuttled down the marble staircase. She was not in the library, nor the conservatory. He stepped out a rear door into a morning fragrant with honeysuckle and so sun-struck it might have been a Monet.

Shielding his eyes from the light, he pivoted.

"What are you looking for?" Rowena called, approaching from the driveway.

"Sunshine like this could blind a man." Her skein of golden hair was tousled, he couldn't help but notice, her cheeks unnaturally flushed.

"I took a walk, such a perfect morning."

"Yes it is—perfect." He took a few strides toward her, wanting to bury his hands in her hair and feel her breath warm the cords of his neck, but she had already opened the door and stood with one sneakered foot on the threshold.

"I could use a bath," she said and slipped hurriedly inside.

The day seemed to dim once she'd gone, and David shut himself inside the library, re-reading old volumes of verse, rehearsing poetic seductions. How much simpler, how touchingly feral, were those faraway nights in Maine, memories now, yet still potent enough to induce a cold sweat. *She walks in beauty like the night...*

He must have dozed. The volume of Byron lay open across his ribs and the prune-like face of Madame Fermat hovered over him.

"Did you not hear the *telephone?* A boy is asking for you."

"Did you catch his name?"

The housekeeper, already at the door, only muttered under her breath.

He picked up the nearest handset. "David Crown here."

"It's Rashid. Just thought I'd say hello."

"What a surprise." David pressed his ear to the receiver, like a doctor probing a heartbeat through a stethoscope. "I wasn't expecting... How have you been?"

"Long story, and there's not much time left on my card."

"Is there somewhere I can call you back? Your uncle's place?"

"I'm not at my uncle's—another long story. Total coincidence, but I think I'm near that village of yours.

Hitched a couple rides and this is where I ended up."

"Near Beautemps?"

"Thought I would stop home, see some old friends."

"Is that a good idea?" David got to his feet, scanned the room for his car keys. "Didn't the authorities nix that sort of thing?"

"Where the hell else am I supposed to go?"

"Is your brother with you?"

"Emile? He split for Barcelona. Met a Spanish babe shoplifting in Uniprix and… you know how that goes."

"We really must talk."

"I've got to get back on the road. People are starting to look at me funny."

"You must come for lunch. I insist. Just tell me where to find you."

"Look, I'm out of minutes…"

In the end Rashid acquiesced, and David drove in all haste to a nearby rest stop, settled him in the passenger seat, and whisked him back to the *Vie Dorée*. It seemed the right thing to do, however awkward or ambiguous the boy's situation. He was even bonier than David remembered him—when had he last had a proper meal?

Madame Fermat met them at the door. "*Monsieur le Maire* came by earlier." Her gaze gravitated without mercy to Rashid's scars. The boy winced and took a step back. Undeterred, the housekeeper inclined toward David's ear and whispered, "An urchin with a face like mincemeat. What business could such a creature have here?"

"Rashid is my guest. He'll be joining us for lunch."

Madame raised the angle of her chin. "No lunch was requested. Your mother eats nothing but chocolates, and *L'Americaine* exists on air."

"Please prepare coffee and sandwiches. We'll be in the conservatory."

Again she tilted toward David and whispered, "Someone ought to keep an eye on him. Shall I call Durand?"

He waved the remark away, took Rashid by the arm, and led him through the shuttered rooms out into the light.

Rashid glanced over a shoulder. "Almost didn't make it past that maid of yours."

"Madame Fermat? It would take three Sumo wrestlers and a pack of Dobermans to replace her. She means well."

"Sure, *habibi*."

"We don't receive many guests."

The boy's smile held a certain acerbity. "No wonder."

David motioned the guest into a seat. "Here she comes now," he whispered and headed to the door, intending to relieve the housekeeper of the silver tea tray. "Thank you, *madame*. I'll do the serving."

Madame Fermat held fast to the tray, walked heavily to the table, and set out the tea service in a precise square before retreating in a sulky silence.

When she had gone, David heaped Rashid's plate and poured his coffee. "So, your brother is gone?"

"For now. Says he'll send for me once he gets a job."

David, having unwittingly financed Emile's desertion, mulled its ramifications. "Does he know you're here?"

"He doesn't even know I'm gone."

Yet.

"No one does," the boy added.

"You're welcome to stay for a few days. Perhaps I can call and speak with your uncle—he's bound to be worried."

"Worried maybe, but not about me. *Mec's* got eight kids and a wife with cancer."

"I see."

"If you'd rather I get lost—" Rashid was already on his feet, poised to flee.

"You're welcome, truly. Sit down. Please." David watched the boy devour the duck paté and pastries with his eyes. "You must be hungry. The road will do that to a man."

The boy, as proud as he was ravenous, sat back down. "I can help out while I'm here."

"You're my guest, Rashid, not a servant."

"Look, this is a big place and your help are a couple of Goths. There must be something that needs doing."

"Let me think about it. In the meantime, enjoy your lunch while I have a quick word with the women of the house." David pushed back his chair.

"I didn't know we had a visitor." Miriam approached with brittle dignity. To David's relief she presented herself fully dressed, cheeks rouged, hair curled in the manner of a '20s flapper. She turned with a regal air to Rashid. "Who might you be, young man?"

"Rashid Jean Hamadi, *à votre disposition*." He bowed and pulled out a chair for the matron.

"I didn't realize Moors were still part of the Commonwealth… impossible to keep up. Are you in oil? Well, you seem a well-bred sort. Make yourself at home. Have you had tea?"

"Coffee, *madame*. May I pour you a cup?"

"Revolting stuff, coffee, and to think it comes from a bean!" Miriam sat down and swiveled her torso to face the young guest. "So, what brings you to the castle?"

If Rashid found the question off-beam, he didn't let on. "I'm a friend of your son."

"Rashid, Rashid… doesn't ring a bell, but Davey can be such a vault. I don't suppose you're a school chum. An employee of the firm, perhaps?"

"Rashid is a personal friend, Mum. We met in Toulouse." The explanation seemed to satisfy her. "He'll be staying with us for a few days while we sort out something more permanent."

"The green room would do nicely—that way we'll be neighbors, my little Moor. You must stop in for a game of pinochle."

David rose and picked up a beat-up gym bag that lay at Rashid's feet. "Come, Rashid, I'll get you settled. Is this all you've brought with you?" The boy, taking a last sip of coffee, nodded. "We'll see you at dinner, Mum."

Rashid bent over Miriam's hand and reverently air-kissed its arthritic knuckles. "*A bientôt*, Madame Crown. I look forward to our card game."

PRIVATE MATTERS

David paced between the green room and his own, silently rehearsing what he would say to Rowena and anticipating her response—a futile exercise. The longer he lived with his young lover, the more opaque her behavior seemed to become. Abandoning caution, resigned to whatever fate held in store, he knocked lightly at the door and stepped inside.

Rowena lay clothed on the bed with her eyes closed and her unruly hair pinwheeled across the pillow. Tempted to stroke the golden strands, he sat down alongside her. "Napping, my rose?"

The corner of her mouth faintly twitched. "Am I late for something?"

"Not at all." David stretched-out full-length and bundled Rowena into his arms. Her skin smelled of mint and talcum powder. "When did we last lie together in the middle of the day? I lost you to that book of yours."

"I lost you—to your *private matters*."

"That's what I'm here to talk with you about. There's a young man downstairs, the same young man who firebombed the synagogue. The younger of the two, Rashid." He felt her tense from the jaw down.

"Here?" She buoyed herself on an elbow, primed to bolt. "Have you called the police?"

"There's no need, no danger," he hastened to reassure her. "Rashid and I have been in touch, ever since... I know this must come as a surprise to you."

She rolled onto her back, crossed her arms in the manner of a Sumerian mummy. "You didn't think I would understand."

"You seemed so keen to have me move on, as if nothing had happened. I couldn't."

"This rift between us—that's when it started, wasn't it? You needed time. I needed *you*."

"You never lost me." He reached out a hand and stroked the sunburnt ellipse of flesh framing her collarbone.

"So, this young man has somehow become a part of your life, of *our* life?"

"He's my concern, not yours. He'll stay for a short while. I would appreciate your treating him cordially until a more practical solution can be found."

"Sweets," she said, turning over and bellying toward him with the lascivious smile that never failed to arouse, "you make me so darn proud. If this boy means something to you, that's enough for me. We're in this together."

David could have wept with gratitude.

"When can I meet him?"

"Dinner soon enough?" David pulled back her mane and kissed the hot pinkness of her neck. "I thought we might get reacquainted."

She rose up like a sleek sea animal and swept him into a tide pool of torrid light and quivering jellyfish. He took air at her lips. Had the walls given way, had the whole of his world been swept into the brine, he could not have stopped kissing her.

CICADAS

Rashid appeared for dinner punctually at seven, wearing a dress shirt and whip-thin leather tie. Moments later, Rowena swept into the room with the animal grace of a woman who knows herself desired.

"Just the three of us," David said and introduced them.

"*Enchanté, madame.*"

His girlfriend, slow to master the French cheek-kissing ritual, greeted the boy with an American-style hug.

Having let Madame Fermat off early, David surveyed the pots and pans left at a low simmer atop the stove.

The houseguest didn't hesitate to roll up his shirtsleeves. "How can I help?"

"Take a seat. Everything's ready." David began filling bowls and walking them to the table. Madame Fermat's inimitable onion soup sent up a piquant bouquet. Rowena popped the cork on a local *Blanc de Blancs*.

"I didn't hear the dinner bell." Miriam, diamonds glittering at her neck, swept into the room in her pom-pom slippers and black silk kimono. Seeing Rashid her crinkled face lit up. "What a coincidence, our meeting again like this. Davey, you remember Mr... the young Moor."

"Rashid, Mum. He's staying with us for a few days."

David raised his glass, intending to propose a toast but finding himself strangely tongue-tied. Rowena queried him with a glance then raised her own glass and said, "To our guest!"

Rashid covered his heart with his hand.

David cut a baguette into ragged slices. "No standing on ceremony."

"I suppose we might put protocol aside for one night,"

concurred Miriam, absently fingering her diamonds.

In unison their four silver spoons dipped into the pungent, oily soup.

"So, my Moor, tell us all about your country."

Rashid wiped his lips on a serviette and replied with perfect courtesy, "You're in my country, *madame*. France. My father was born in Algeria, but I've never been there."

"*Ah*." Miriam turned to David, "How terribly interesting, don't you think?" Before David could respond, she placed a withered hand on Rashid's wrist and went on, "Davey's father was a very successful man, you know. What does your father do?"

"Not much. He was laid-off a few years ago from the factory."

Miriam softly clucked her tongue. "Are you seeing anyone?"

"Like a shrink, you mean?"

"No, my Moor, I was referring to a girl, a special friend, but perhaps you're too engrossed in your studies to think about romance."

"A man is never too busy to think about romance."

Rowena laughed (David loved her laugh, wide and loon-like). "In books, perhaps. I've heard you like books."

"That's how Rowena and I met," David interjected, "in a library."

"Rowena?" parroted Miriam, lapsing into stony puzzlement.

"My girlfriend, Mum." Having lost all appetite, David pushed aside his plate, took Rowena's hand, and recalled winter mornings spent digging out from under four feet of snow, nights huddled before the woodstove, and the days, icy cascades of desire, interned within the library.

"David was searching for the meaning of life," Rowena said. "He'd spend hours wandering through the stacks touching bindings. Some patrons did that, touch." She took a sip of wine and set down her glass. The coral-colored imprint of her lips remained on the rim.

Miriam turned with stiff majesty to Rashid. "If you're here to seek a position, we may be able to use you in the Diplomatic Corps."

The boy, a model of courtliness, bowed in his seat. "I would be honored, Your Highness. There's nothing I desire more than to serve my queen."

"Arrange it, Davey, won't you? Nothing too taxing." The matron rolled her serviette and drew it through an engraved silver ring. She touched a lacquered fingernail to her lower lip. "Where did you say you were from?"

"It's late, Mum." David rose and draped an arm about her shrunken frame. "We could all use a rest."

The moon had flooded in, casting Rowena's face into shadow. Without warning she bolted to her feet, steadied her chair, and yanked shut the east-facing door.

"These cicadas are driving me up the wall," she said.

And then the others heard them too, and there was no remedy but to shut the windows, all of them.

LIONEL LAYS DOWN THE LAW

It being a Saturday, Lionel slept in and awoke to find Laura hurriedly pulling on a slinky knit dress far too formal for a day at the lake.

"Going somewhere?"

Dropping to her knees and feeling under the bed for her shoes, she replied, "Foussier called. He's been asked on short notice to give a paper at Oxford."

"But you've worked every day this week." Lionel sounded like a petulant child and knew it.

His wife paused, reached out a hand to stroke his

cheek. "But *Capitaine*, you have work of your own to do. Your desk is piled ear-high."

He needed no reminder. What he needed was his wife, gloriously nude, spooned close beside him in the clammily cold bed. "Just make sure the old skinflint pays you overtime."

Laura bent down and kissed him on the brow. "I'll be home early, *chèri*," she said and glided out the door with her hips swaying to a beat so maddeningly hers.

Lionel went about his day in a glum torpor—signing papers, shredding papers... the wasteful, endless busy work spawned by a bureaucracy he detested and yet served. Would Foussier and his ilk rid the world of such anachronisms? Would they leave something more equitable, less soul-sapping in its place? Laura seemed to think so.

Having burrowed through the paper mountain to some semblance of order, Lionel left the *mairie* and headed across the square to the village's one bistro, intending to reward himself with a *café au lait*. He might have taken coffee in his own home, away from his constituents and their petty demands, but "being seen" came with the office, and given voters' burgeoning shift to the Right he could ill afford to hide.

Midway a voice called, "Lionel, over here!"

David rose from a sidewalk table, and daubing his lips on a serviette, walked briskly toward him. David's American girlfriend stayed behind with a scar-faced young stranger in the gangster-style clothes then fashionable among adolescents of a certain social class.

David clapped him on the back with more than his usual exuberance. "I was hoping we would run into you."

Lionel glanced again in the direction of the dark young stranger.

"We have a house guest for a few days, unexpected.

You'll never guess—"

"The delinquent from the synagogue? Here?"

"Rashid. Out of the blue, but he fits in somehow. It's wonderful having a young person around, don't you think?"

Lionel draped an arm about the beaming Englishman and lowered his voice. "David, David… there are legalities to consider. The boy is a minor, a minor with a police record. What does his guardian say?"

David looked stung. "Come now, Lionel, the boy arrived only yesterday."

"Apply logic: You're a man of means, the sort of man people like these prey upon. Protect yourself."

"Rashid gets on so well with mother."

Lionel fought the urge to take David by the shoulders and shake him. "Have you heard anything I've said?"

"I know you mean well, Lionel, but the boy has no one. His own brother abandoned him."

"That should tell you something." The boy swiveled to look at him, a look of curiosity, innocent enough, but his scars told a different story. "*Attends*, I have a friend in juvenile services, a hardline child advocate, but she knows her job. I'll have her call you."

"No harm in talking." David gestured toward the table. "Now come, join us."

"I was just heading home," Lionel fibbed, weary suddenly and wanting nothing more than to close a door behind him and sink into his faithful old armchair.

"Stop by the house," David made him promise and hurried back to his bookish lover and the inscrutable young ex-con whose face Lionel was not likely to forget.

DOMESTIC ARRANGEMENTS

Rashid made the perfect houseguest—undemanding,

courteous to a fault—but his presence seemed to unsettle Madame Fermat and to drive Durand to new levels of insolence. David could skirt the issue with his housekeeper but not with the gardener, whose cooperation he sought to enlist.

"Rashid would like to lend a hand around the grounds. Few hours a day, whatever needs doing."

Durand's lower lip puffed up like a blowfish. "I don't need a hand."

"There must be something you can let him do. The boy wants to be helpful."

"Is the *monsieur* not satisfied with my service?"

"You're a fine gardener, Durand." One had only to glance at the grounds, verdant and fruitful, to appreciate the curmudgeon's uncanny talent.

"Then let me do my work," the gardener snapped. "A boy like that is more trouble than he's worth. Where did he come from, anyway?"

"Rashid is my guest. Be reasonable, for mercy's sake, and give the boy a few chores."

The gardener, grit-toothed, rammed his spade into the earth. "*Comme vous voulez.* Just don't expect me to fraternize. You may pay my wages, but I am my own man."

David nodded and walked away, telling himself that his servants would soon grow accustomed to Rashid, perhaps even grow fond of him. The boy had the good manners they lacked and something far more precious. His company, the pleasure it gave, made the *Vie Dorée* feel like home—the home David had longed for all his life.

THE PROPOSITION

"You must be Crown, *n'est-ce pas?*"

David stood sifting envelopes beside the mailbox at the

foot of the driveway. "I'm sorry, have we met?" A woman sidled up to him, so close he could smell her drugstore perfume and underarm musk. Blond and fair with the prematurely gnarled brow of the careworn, her clothes too tight and her manner loose, she could not have been from Beautemps.

She stepped in closer. "My son lives with you. I am Madame Hamadi."

David, hoping to hide his shock, assumed a casual tone. "If you've come to see your son, he's gone out. I could have him call you or you're welcome to leave a note."

"It's you I'm here to see, Crown," she said and started up the driveway. "Can we talk somewhere private? Very private."

Durand puttered nearby, pruning the hedgerow and casting sideways glances. Rowena had taken Rashid berry picking in the adjacent woods. Jockeying for distance, David walked reluctantly toward the conservatory. "If I'm not mistaken, the court has forbidden you access to your son."

"If I'm not mistaken, my son is a minor and pedophilia can get your name smeared across the media awful bad. Emile can smell a pervert a mile off. You might fool your cop friend but not my boys and me."

David stopped and faced her squarely. "I've done nothing but try to be a friend to your son. He came to me in need and I hadn't the heart to put him out."

"I like a man with heart," she said, her voice gone breathy. "Nothing turns me on like heart."

"Have you come to blackmail me?"

"That or to get it on with you. You're kind of cute, Mr. Moneybags Crown, you know that?" She reached out and fingered his belt buckle.

"Not interested."

"Fine, faggot, then just give me the money."

"For drugs?"

She fished a filterless cigarette out from behind her ear and waited for him to light it. He didn't. "Why are you so down on me?"

"You're a mother, for godsake. Your sons need you. Get yourself some help."

"Why don't you help me? You like Rashid well enough—why not me? Same genes."

Her hand plunged down the front of his pants. Stunned mute, he grabbed hold of her wrist and gingerly lifted.

"Prefer a more delicate approach?" she cooed and flashed her tongue.

"I'm going to have to ask you to leave."

"Stop being such a prude, *chéri*, and let me make you feel good. All over. No one does what I do. I get inside a man…"

David glanced toward Durand who had repositioned himself at the shed, the better to spy on them. "Madame Hamadi, please don't force me to call the police."

"You've got a shitload more to lose than I do, Crown. Watch yourself, *eh?* You're no match for me. I know where you live."

"Your son is well, Madame Hamadi, not that you asked. Now get out."

She backed unsteadily away, cursing him as she went. "I know what you're up to, faggot…"

David let himself into the chateau through a side door and stood, back against the jamb, feeling his heart pound like a meat mallet.

THE OUTING

David knocked at the door of the green room, hoping

to have a word with Rashid before breakfast, but the boy did not answer. David opened the door and called Rashid's name—still no answer. He was about to retrace his steps when a door at the opposite end of the hallway opened and Rashid stepped out.

"Looking for me?" he said.

"As a matter of fact…" David had slept poorly and awoken determined to resolve the legal ambiguities inherent in his relationship with the young guest. "I've had a talk with a woman in family services, a specialist in situations like yours—"

"You're sending me back to my uncle?"

"Not immediately, and not permanently. There are ways of changing your status, but these things take time."

"Just say it, you're sending me away."

Miriam—coiffed, perfumed and dressed in street clothes—stepped out from her bedroom. "I'm ready for our date, my Moor."

David's jaw dropped.

"I told your mother about the wildflowers that bloom along the banks of the lake," the boy explained. "I offered to escort her there."

Exuding youthful excitement, Miriam took Rashid's arm. "I fancy an ice cream."

David, who had been trying for months to convince his mother to leave the chateau and get to know the village, stepped aside to let them pass. "Spot-on. Here, let me treat." He held out a twenty-euro note.

"Come with us, Davey, no use your staying indoors on a splendid day like this."

"Of course, Mum, I'd love to—if it's all right with Rashid."

The two men high-fived then positioned themselves to either side of Miriam. Arm-in-arm, they descended the marble staircase and passed into the sunlit foyer.

"*Attendez!*" Madame Fermat stormed out from the kitchen, a tea towel in her hands and a smear of orange marmalade across her open mouth. "But you have not had your breakfast."

"A deviation from routine, *madame.*"

"Anarchy," uttered the housekeeper and stamped back to her post.

"Insufferable old killjoy." Miriam, squinting, drew open the oversized front door. "Come, lads, let's see what mischief we can get up to."

Morning Dip

David and Rowena's morning dips in the hot tub resumed, a second honeymoon of sorts. The couple's ardor seemed to revive with the arrival of Rashid, with their shared interest in the boy's welfare.

"Race you to the tub," said Rowena, bolting from bed flushed and unabashedly nude.

"I'll just throw on some clothes." David grabbed a pair of swim trunks from the chaise.

"No, come as you are."

Not wanting to appear prudish or worse, old, David capered after her to the door, along the hallway and down the stairs. Terrified of getting caught, he labored to match Rowena's airy abandon—she, a nymph, and he merely ridiculous.

"Relax," she chided, reaching the tub a scant few seconds before him and plunging in her leg.

David hung back, glancing up nervously at the bedroom windows.

"Mary, mother of God!" Rowena leapt from the tub, took a few one-footed hops, and fell writhing to the lawn.

David dropped to his knees beside her.

"Stay back! Don't touch me! The water, it's eating through my skin. Quick, get the garden hose."

"But I tested the water only yesterday."

"Get the hose, get the hose… Jesus, I'm on fire. Get the goddam hose!"

He scrabbled to his feet, raced to the nearest tap, and pulled the hose to where Rowena, convulsing, lay. He doused her hard and long, and watched in horror as her burnt leg blistered and turned the color of raw liver.

"Don't stop, Jesus don't stop!"

"We need to get you to the ER." Obvious, but how does a naked middle-aged man gather up a flailing bundle of pain; how does he present himself at an urban hospital with his scrotum sheepishly drooping?

"Keep it coming, don't stop…"

"Davey, you rascal, what sort of prank is this?" As if the situation were not sufficiently dire, there stood his mother, wide-eyed, stifling a giggle. "And that naked woman—in broad daylight, and isn't she a tad young for you?"

"Listen carefully, Mum. I need you to go upstairs into my bedroom and bring us some clothes—trousers, shoes… Clothes, can you remember that?"

The mirth drained from Miriam's expression. "But she's crying. What did you do to her?"

"Mum, please, just bring the clothes." To his infinite relief she turned and walked toward the house. David could do no more than train the hose on Rowena's ravaged leg, scarred now. "My rose, my beautiful rose, I can't bear to see you hurt."

And then Miriam was back, holding out an assortment of mismatched shoes, jockey shorts, a bathrobe and David's panama. He pulled on the shorts, draped Rowena in the robe, and mentally measured the distance to his estate car—

too far. "Get Rashid," he ordered his mother. "Get the *Moor*. Tell him to bring the car keys."

Together David and Rashid carried the blanched, limp body of Rowena to the car and arranged her, ensconced in ice packs, on the back seat. She had closed her eyes and gone silent, still.

The boy asked no questions, only looked on knowingly, as if such domestic atrocities were commonplace. "Acid," he pronounced, closing the car door.

"You'll take care of Miriam?"

The boy nodded and waved him off.

If the sun rose, David did not see it. It was the longest drive of his life, and the darkest. At the far end a battery of fluorescent lights swallowed up what remained of his self-possession. He watched Rowena's mutilated body glide away on a chrome trolley and drove his fist, iron-like in its fury, through the nearest wall.

666 RUE PARADIS

The Hamadi flat was not difficult to find. David had seen the address on forms littering Lebrun's desk. One does not easily forget a number like 666, nor a slum street called "Paradise."

The housing estate lay on the outskirts of Toulouse, not far from the salvage yard David had visited only a few months earlier. The building itself, a blockish high-rise crisscrossed by laundry lines and wreathed in graffiti, was surrounded by asphalt parking lots, which doubled as ball courts. Teenagers clustered outside smoking, listening to music, playing soccer. They looked him over—some with curiosity, others with suspicion—and then coolly turned their backs.

David entered a shadowy vestibule, hot, smelling of

sewage, and mounted a narrow flight of stairs. At the top stood 666, its faux bronze placard come loose from the black, peeling door. He knocked and stood back, bracing.

The door opened a fraction of an inch and an eye peered through the crack. "What are you doing here?" The breathy voice of Madame Hamadi. "Wait for me downstairs, over by the dumpsters."

He did not have long to wait. Madame Hamadi, clad in pop-beads and Spandex, seemed eager to pick up the thread of their aborted first meeting.

"What I've come to say is very simple. Stay away from my home; stay away from the people I love; just stay the hell away."

She pouted and looked for a moment like a schoolgirl sent to bed without her milk and cookies.

"You know why I'm here."

"I assumed you had second thoughts and wanted a little..." She ran her tongue along her plum-painted lips.

"Fifty liters of acid." The lab analysis surpassed his worst fear. "Sulfuric acid, industrial strength. From the *Grande Paroisse*, correct?" A thriving chemical plant employing hundreds of locals.

"I'm not saying I did it, and I'm not saying I didn't. Kind of clever, though, wasn't it?"

"Clever? You call scarring an innocent woman for life *clever?*"

"Must have smarted like hell. I've heard that it does."

"You hurt the wrong person. If you need to hurt someone, here I am. Let's get this over with here and now."

"Must have cost you an arm and a leg, no pun intended, to clean something like that up. Hazardous waste and all."

Indeed it had, not to mention the inflated surcharge for performing the removal by night.

"I don't give a damn about the money. Have you no shame, no remorse?" She smiled, a bitter little smile that accentuated the hard angle of her jaw. "Were you human once?"

"I'm an addict, Crown, and addicts are human in the worst sort of way."

"Stay away from my girlfriend."

She sidled up to him, rubbing her pushed-up breasts against his flank. "What's it worth to you? Cause you see, safety isn't given, it's bought. I've got friends in the protection business."

"Don't push me. Don't force me to…"

"To what, *chéri?* There's nothing you can do to me that hasn't already been done. You're the vulnerable one, the one shitting his pants, and you ought to be. I may not have your pedigree, Crown, but I've got friends. There are people who appreciate my particular gifts."

To stand there and trade threats would accomplish nothing. "Rashid is getting on well in Beautemps. Don't ruin it for him."

For a moment her schoolgirl face returned, and David dared to hope that maternity might restore reason. "I don't suppose he talks about me?"

"Give him a reason to."

She seemed to mull this. "Who are we kidding, Crown? It's too damn late—for me, and for you. There's no going home to your snug little world. Watch your back." She turned and sauntered off, weaving unsteadily through the brimming dumpsters.

David drew out a handkerchief, and covering his nose and mouth, headed at a trot for the Volvo. He got in, locked all the doors, and drove to the exit. Distracted by a neon sign flashing *Lingerie Luxe,* he didn't see who tossed the beer bottle at his windshield—he saw only the bottle, coming toward him as if in slow motion, glinting like hellfire. How much petrol did it hold? How deadly would be its blast upon impact? Would it boil his brain, as Lebrun had so graphically described? Would he die instantly or survive to smell his flesh char?

The bottle struck and fell away, harmlessly shattering on the asphalt.

Exhaling, David floored the accelerator.

DAMAGE CONTROL

The flowers and shrubs Durand had planted in the vicinity of the hot tub quickly withered. The old gardener paced the perimeter of the empty tub, cursing and shaking his head.

"That area has been contaminated," David cautioned. "Best to avoid it and not replant."

"You've killed my peonies, my snapdragons…"

"Plant over there." David pointed at random to a remote swath of lawn.

"My lemon balm, my chamomile…"

"Plant all you want, just not near the tub."

The gardener raised a stubby index finger. "I warned you about that boy."

"Rashid has nothing to do with this. The error was mine. If you need to blame someone, blame me."

David walked hurriedly toward the chateau and let himself in a side door. The room was in perfect order; sunlight streamed through the windows. In a corner, resting on a fainting couch with her wounded leg stretched out in front of her, Rowena looked up from the book she had been reading—Ibsen, it may have been—and said, "I've told Rashid it was just a mix-up with the chemicals. He seemed to buy the story."

David kept his doubts to himself. "What's important is that the boy feel welcome here."

"Your friend Lionel is bound to find out the truth; he knows everything that goes on in this village."

David perched alongside his girlfriend, savoring her nearness and the tacit conspiracy into which they ventured with righteous sangfroid. "Lionel is a reasonable man, but he's not keen on Rashid. Never has been."

"I like the kid. He does us all good. You won't send him away, will you?"

"I don't want to, but what kind of man am I if I can't keep you safe?" He glanced with a pang at her bandaged leg.

"The best kind, man enough." She drew him toward her with a tenderness he had only known in dreams. "You said it yourself, safety is an illusion. We mustn't let ourselves be intimidated."

"If anyone were to hurt you again… I may not be able to restrain myself next time."

"You'll do the right thing, sweets. You always do."

David wasn't so sure.

An Education

Rowena took two painkillers, drew on a gauzy pair of drawstring pants, and allowed David to carry her down the marble staircase—as Rhett Butler had once done for Scarlet O'Hara in a mansion not so very different from the *Vie Dorée*. David may not have had Rhett's swagger, but to a bookworm from rural Maine woozily adrift on Vicodin he made a more than adequate leading man.

"Rashid should be down any moment. He's always so punctual."

David set her gently on her feet. "Are you sure you're up to this?"

It had been Rashid's idea, a sunset picnic at the lake. Miriam had agreed at once. Rendered girlish, she unearthed a parasol from one of her cavernous closets and pulled on long satin gloves.

"I'll be fine. It's your mother I worry about, her sudden departures into the ether."

"Leave her to me. Leave everything to me."

Rashid appeared at the landing with Miriam on his arm, the two amiably chatting.

"Davey, the young Moor has just been telling me the most charming stories about a place called Paradise—Paradise, can you imagine?"

David grimaced but said nothing.

"Something wrong, sweets?"

Miriam unfurled her parasol and descended the staircase with brittle majesty.

It might all have been make-believe—the chateau, the gloves, the Queen Mother and her exotic courtier—if not for Rowena's mangled leg, softly throbbing beneath its gauze shroud. "Did you pack the wine?"

"Champagne, my rose. Everything's already in the Volvo, set to go."

David drove to the river, and they walked along the bank to where the trees parted affording a stunning view of the setting sun. Rashid spread out a Tartan blanket and helped Miriam settle herself on a cushion.

"How I love picnics! Willy never had time for them, and how he hated insects—ants, caterpillars… anything that crawled."

"Bugs are just living their lives, your Ladyship, same as us."

"I'd never thought of it that way," she said, gazing at the boy as if he had imparted the Eleventh Commandment. "They're so puny, after all."

David took plates, glasses and cutlery from the hamper and set them out. Rowena uncorked the champagne.

"The school term will be starting again soon," David thought aloud. "Has your uncle registered you at a *lycée?*"

"He'd rather I work, and maybe he's right. The schools suck anyway."

"There are other ways to get an education."

"Like what?" asked the boy with evident skepticism.

"Why, we could homeschool you, David and I." Rowena, having planted the idea, quickly warmed to it. "I'm decent at math and history, and David—weren't you a wiz at geography?"

David had on his English face, impossible to read. "I got by."

"We could find out which textbooks are current and brush-up."

Rashid, his excitement uncontainable, blurted, "I could perfect my English and read the great philosophers. I'll study hard. All day and all night, if that's what it takes."

Miriam, shielding her eyes, pointed to the western horizon, where a dazzling sunset cast out beams of red and gold. "Splendid! Splendid!"

"Quiche anyone?" David cut generous wedges and passed them around.

"So," said Rowena, the champagne adding a heady effervescence to her narcotic torpor, "when do we start?"

A pained expression settled on David's brow. "I'll need to consult with someone about this—not that I'm opposed to homeschooling, in principle. But these aren't our decisions to make. Rashid has a family, don't forget."

"Some family, mister."

Miriam gave the boy an affectionate ribbing. "Buck up, my Moor. People are starving in Sudan—or do I mean Somalia?"

A gaggle of geese fluttered up from the lake and wobbled in the direction of the diners' heaped plates. Rowena threw them crumbs. David skimmed a pebble along the lake's surface then handed one to the boy.

"Not to worry, Rashid, we'll look into it. We'll sort something out."

DAVID SEES YELLOW

As summer waned the Atlantic seemed to draw nearer. David took a walk along the river, a meandering walk that carried him past the windmill and then along the track that bordered Swijdendorp's farm. Normally he would have cut through the village on the homeward leg, but roused by the salt-stung air and cooling shade he kept to the perimeter and approached the *Vie Dorée* from behind, entering though the conservatory and making his way toward the kitchen for a glass of water.

He didn't see his mother at first—she had to have been in the parlor. He heard the rasp of chair legs and then a crash. More curious than alarmed, he crossed the foyer. From the doorway he watched Miriam kneel on the crewel rug, nudge aside an overturned lamp, and wrestle with a Queen Anne armchair twice her size, inching it in his direction.

"Mum?"

"Willy?" Was she seeing ghosts? "Thank goodness you're home!" Winded, she motioned him over and kicked off her pumps. "Come, give me a hand with this. We need to barricade the doors."

David froze on the threshold. "Barricade?"

She raised an index finger to the bow of her lips and whispered, "They're back."

"Who—who's back?"

"*Them.* Hurry, they could be nearby, in the bushes,

anywhere. It's that Fermat woman—how else could they have found us out?"

"What are you talking about?"

She led him to the window and peeled back the draperies. "Look, it's starting all over again."

The day had remained flawless. No obvious object of dread in sight. She pointed and his gaze skimmed along Monsieur Durand's privet, beyond the gate, then down to the wall of names that formed part of the war memorial. Scrawled across it in piss yellow paint was a swastika, the first of several sloppily painted in a descending line.

"*Yellow*," she uttered. Her hand grabbed at the fabric of his polo shirt and tugged toward the center of the room. "Come, we don't have much time." She applied herself yet again to the armchair, dipping at the knee to lean her shoulder into it and to push with all her weight.

"So, you think we can hold them off like this?"

"Not for long. We'll have to find a hiding place."

"That will take some thought."

As they maneuvered the armchair into place David heard Madame Fermat's moped putter up the driveway. In a moment, he knew, the housekeeper would round the chateau and let herself in the kitchen door.

"We had better go upstairs," he hastened to say. "No hiding places down here, I've already looked."

"But the doors! There are so many of them." She huffed across the rug and braced her bulk against the settee. "Come on, get a hold."

He heard Madame Fermat's clogs before her person tramped into view. Miriam, swerving toward the parlor door, aimed an accusing finger. "It's her! The filthy informer turned us in."

The housekeeper, still tying on her apron, cocked a penciled brow. "*C'est quoi, son problème?*"

A direct appeal seemed his only hope: *"S'il vous plait, laissez nous.* For mercy's sake, can't you just back off for once?"

"It's her," his mother insisted, "I'm telling you. She speaks their language. I've heard her."

Muttering under her breath the Alsatian marched toward the fallen lamp.

"Stop her!" cried Miriam.

What happened next David couldn't say with certainty. One moment a brass candlestick holder glinted in Miriam's hand, and the next Madame Fermat crashed to the stone floor atop her wood-soled clogs and lay there moaning. He didn't recall seeing Rowena enter the room, but at the height of the fray she seemed to fill it, encircling Miriam with her arms.

David crouched down beside the housekeeper and scanned her face and arms for any obvious injuries—none. He palpated her legs. Straining to raise her head from the floor she pushed him away. Pointing to David's mother with her chin and miming the turning of a screwdriver, she pronounced, *"Cinglé!"*

Rowena, her back turned, restored the candlestick to its place above the hearth. "She's not crazy, she's *ill.*" Her words brought the room to stillness. David's mind, groping without object, measured distances: Miriam listing to one side of the parlor, Madame Fermat's inert body sprawled on the other, and Rowena in-between, clearing a path through the mayhem. He bent down to straighten the rug. "Leave that and get Rashid," Rowena said. She pivoted toward him, her face pale, pale as cream, in contrast to the red stain that flared beneath her throat.

"But you're hurt."

She touched an innocent finger to the blood.

"I can't bear to see you hurt—again."

A rational man would have proceeded from A to B to C, picking up the pieces. A rational man would have gone for the first aid kit, urged calm, taken charge. Order was paramount but his mind resisted linear thinking.

"I'll call an ambulance," Rowena said and left the room.

Miriam gazed after her. "She's cross with me, isn't she?"

"Sit down, Mum."

"I have the most terrible feeling—what's that woman doing on the floor?"

"Sit down. Please. Stay there. I'll be back."

A rational man would not have left the scene, but adrenaline took over carrying him down the driveway, along the defaced wall, through the square... Only at the *Rue Moulin à Huile* did he notice the orange gumdrop sun overhanging the horizon and the giddy light it cast on the rooftops. He noticed and walked on, ruled by his legs. They carried him to Lionel's gate and up his front path. David had no will to stop them. Before he reached the doorstep, Lionel beckoned from a lawn chair and said, "Have I forgotten a match?"

"No match."

Lionel tossed aside the *Midi Libre* he had been reading. "*Ça va*, David?"

"Come with me."

"*A votre service, citoyen.*" Yawning he lumbered to his feet.

David turned on his heels and began to retrace his steps back to the square then left along the two-lane blacktop. Lionel followed, pausing once or twice to pocket a discarded drinking straw or lottery ticket. He wore rubberized sandals that clacked against the soles of his feet. As they passed from sunlight to shade the war memorial came into view.

David pointed. "Look. Do you see that? Do you see?"

"*Calme-toi, mon vieux.*"

He strode ahead and planted himself in front of the swastika. "There are no *banlieues* in Beautemps, correct? So, *Monsieur le Maire*, how do you explain this—this tribute?"

Lionel, his back to the wall, gazed along the outbound road. "It is tourist season. We have had an unusually high number of German visitors this summer."

"*Ah*, Germans."

"Germans, Russians…."

"Who are you blaming, the Germans or the Russians?"

"I was merely thinking aloud. I blame no one. I will deal with it."

"Its placement is brilliant, right where my mother couldn't miss seeing it. Do you have any idea the effect it had on her, a woman who gave birth to her first son in a bomb shelter, a woman who lost half her family to Hitler's gas chambers?"

"Most unfortunate, but a coincidence."

"Miriam isn't the only casualty. Madame Fermat has had a fall. An ambulance is on its way."

Before the mayor could react to the news, a low moan issued from the nearby shrubbery. Without exchanging a word, the two men dropped to their knees and burrowed into the dense, overgrown foliage.

"Rashid!" cried Lionel.

David's charge—one eye swollen, a fresh gash across his forehead—shambled to his feet mumbling apologies. "I tried to stop them, *habibi*, I tried…"

"Who did this?"

"Two men with paint cans—one had the paint, the other a hunting rifle."

"What sort of men?"

"The sort you see playing boules in the square. Old *mecs*."

"Then you can identify them?" Lionel interjected.

Rashid waved the question away, a flat negative. "They had handkerchiefs covering their faces and caps on their heads. Hunting caps."

"And they spoke in French?"

"What else would they speak? Like I told you, they were from around here."

Lionel's back hunched as if the cross of Calvary had been strapped to it. "*C'est la cata complète!*"

"Why is that ambulance taking so long? The boy needs to be seen to."

"I don't need any doctor. I've gotten worse from my old man. Let me paint that wall for you before your mother sees it."

"She already has. She thinks she's about to be rounded up and hauled off to a camp."

"David, David… you're overwrought. Let me get you a brandy."

"I'm overwrought and I'll stay overwrought. Is it me or have the French forgotten? There was such a thing as Vichy, was there not? Anti-Semitism is not some imported commodity."

Lionel swung a pointed finger in the direction of the emblem. "*That* is not French."

Rashid drew himself up like a monument to grit. "It may not be the France you know, mister, but it's plenty French to me."

The mayor clenched his fists and said nothing.

"I'm sorry, David, I tried to stop them."

"You've done nothing wrong, Rashid." He took the boy by the arm, such a bony arm and yet solid as a trestle. "Come, I could use your help with Miriam."

Lionel drew an audible breath. "You deal with your mother, I'll deal with the rest."

David turned away and the knot of rage in his chest came undone.

"You take this too personally," Lionel said, sounding anything but detached himself.

"How would you have me take it?" David's hands rose like piqued jays. "Hate is entirely personal. Hate lodges in the gut."

A rational man would have cut his losses, but not David. A man with glass shards in his belly is beyond calculating loss or gain. He turned his back on Lionel and trudged up the driveway toward the *Vie Dorée*, dreading what he would find there. He needn't have. In his absence Rowena had settled Miriam into bed and dispatched Madame Fermat to hospital. She had restored the parlor to pristine normality, doctored herself, had even put on music—Ravel, it may have been.

Then she turned to Rashid. "Have you a headache, double vision?"

Again the boy refused medical care and walked a straight line to prove his essential soundness. Rowena dressed his wounded eye, and the boy excused himself and hurried off to look in on Miriam.

Oddly numb, weary in a way he had never before known, David touched a timid finger to Rowena's chin. "Are you all right?" he said and froze, unable to take her in his arms.

"Don't worry about me." She walked toward the staircase with a steadiness that put him to shame.

"But I'd like to do something. For you."

Her lips drew up on one side (if he hadn't known better, he might have thought she was smirking). "I'm the least of your problems," she reminded him and went upstairs.

Left alone in the parlor, he retrieved a pair of field glasses and positioned himself beside a front-facing window.

Pulling back the draperies, training the lens on the war memorial, he watched as Lionel reached into a bucket and extracted a swelled, foaming sponge. His big-knuckled hands moving in all directions, he ran the sponge over the spray-painted yellow affront. A bevy of children clustered about him. Lionel appeared to be speaking to them as he worked. His yachting cap changed tilt, assuming an angle at once rakish and perilous. David could have wept.

LEBRUN RETURNS

Was David surprised to find Jacques Lebrun on his doorstep the following evening? Does a barn owl clinging to a tall, tenuous twig anticipate the mistral?

"*Alors*, Crown, we meet again and under circumstances that would make a stone weep."

David showed him into the library, a room that with its thousands of volumes of collected wisdom imposed a certain decorum. "I didn't realize Beautemps was your turf."

"It isn't," Lebrun said, dropped into the nearest chair, and clamped his motorcycle helmet to the armrest. "Our mutual friend borrowed me from my unit. Seems my boss owed him a favor."

"It's not like Lionel to involve outsiders."

"This isn't your usual village mischief. *Merde*, you're a magnet for melodrama—sabotaged by neo-Nazis, your maid in hospital, your mother gone off the deep end... and let's not forget your little pal Rashid, who just happens to find himself at the crime scene at the very moment the alleged vandals raise their vile paintbrushes."

"What are you implying?"

"The timing is too perfect. And consider the circumstances: Life deals the boy another hard knock; he shows up on your doorstep; the village lets him know he's not welcome—"

David's hand came down on the desk edge and rebounded shoulder-high. "He was welcome in this home."

Lebrun remained businesslike. "I was speaking of your housekeeper, the gardener, and other old-timers of their ilk. You said it yourself, the boy is sensitive. He had to have felt their disapproval. What better way to expose these people for what they are, to get back at them?"

"But he was injured."

"Not badly. His wounds could have been self-inflicted."

David replayed the scene in memory: the confrontation at the war memorial, Rashid's wan cry from the bushes, his bloodied face... "I don't want to hear anymore, Lebrun. The boy has been victimized."

"That may be—or not. I'm on your side, Crown, always have been."

A man backed into a corner needs to trust someone. "I had a visit from Rashid's mother not long ago. She wanted money. Things got unpleasant."

"How did she know the kid was here?"

"Emile. Apparently, he saw a letter I had written to Rashid and—"

"Don't tell me he tried to blackmail you, too?"

"Not exactly."

The veins rose at Lebrun's temples and faintly pulsed. "Why didn't you call me? *Merde*. I hope you didn't give-in to the junkie's demands?"

"I did not." Watching the anger shift to the lieutenant's eyes, David decided to keep the rest of the story to himself, to downplay its more sinister aspects. "She made threats, unloaded a few insults, and that was that. I didn't want to overreact and besides, I was in a touchy spot myself, harboring a minor."

"*C'est vrai*," pronounced the copper, "touchier than you know." He got to his feet and paced taking his helmet with him, palming its crown as one might a crystal ball. "They act as one, Arab families. It's their clan mentality. If they did this, you can bet your eye teeth that Rashid was in cahoots with them."

"Look, Lebrun, I wouldn't presume to tell you how to do your job—"

"Then don't." The two men eyed each other, their pittance of affection spent. "Let me do some poking around and see what I come up with. In the meantime, I would count the spoons if I were you."

David followed the lieutenant out and watched him mount his Triumph with a toreador's aplomb and lope down the driveway. He had not gone far when old Brioche, trailing a red leather leash, intersected his path. Amused by the incursion Lebrun closed in, cutting circles around the spaniel. He repeated the stunt several times, upping his speed until the aged canine could no longer walk a straight line but had to choose a new direction every few steps. The motorcycle revved, the gears ground, and Lebrun taunted, "Watch your toes, *mon pote.*"

David was already sprinting toward the cycle with his arms flailing. "Leave that dog alone! Can't you see he's mortified? Damn you, Lebrun."

The copper, deaf within his helmet, waved a hand and sped off, slamming the horn until it wailed.

THE TEA PARTY

Miriam shut herself away after Madame Fermat's fall. Several times a day Rowena would press an ear to the closed door of her bedroom. She had read about the elderly smothering in their own turtlenecks, drowning in birdbaths, walking naked into traffic… there was no end to the ways people chose to die.

"Tea, Mrs. Crown?"

Miriam sat up in bed, propped against a tower of pillows. "David's friend, isn't it? We don't get many visitors anymore. That Fermach woman ran them off with her atrocious scones."

"I live here with your son."

"Giddy aunt! David playing away?"

"I'll just pour you a cup."

"But you must join me." She pointed to a curio cabinet. "Take your pick. I've always been partial to Wedgewood."

Rowena took a cup and saucer from the display and half filled it.

"Pull up a chair, dear."

There was only the vanity seat, more a tuffet than a chair. "Would you like to go down to the conservatory? There's more light."

"All this sunshine gets on one's nerves after awhile." Miriam pinced two saccharine tablets with a tiny pair of silver tongs."

"Has Rashid been in to see you?"

"Rashid… I don't believe I know anyone by that name." Her gaze absently drifted. "Nasty rash you've got on your leg—or is it a burn?"

Rowena reached on reflex for the hem of her pant leg and tugged it down. "It's nothing. A little accident."

"Weren't you writing something?"

"The story of Charlotte Corday."

"That cabaret singer Prince Phillip was so crazy about?"

"I think you're confusing her with someone."

"What's there to say about a tart?" She set down her cup and saucer and retied the bow that clasped her bed jacket.

"Mrs. Crown, about your son-—"

"Don't tell me he's decided to leave his wife for you?"

"David has been divorced for a decade."

She lay silent for a moment, smiling into vacant space. "Such an affectionate little boy."

Rowena began to gather up the tea things.

Miriam, repositioning her cushions, rolled in Rowena's direction, "If you're feeling as if you've failed my son in some way, you're not alone."

"He needs something I can't give him."

"Naturally, dear. When a man stops lying to himself, he had better expect to pay the piper." She took the remote control from beneath her pillow, switched on the TV, and hit mute. Her red-rimmed eyes fixed on the screen and Rowena noticed for the first time how close in color they were to David's, the blue of rough seas. "You know, dear, something isn't right. Something's off, terribly—don't tell me it isn't."

"Everything will be okay." Rowena took Miriam's empty cup and placed it on the tray. She took her hand.

"Promise you won't tell Davey? He can be such a worry guts."

Whatever promise Rowena might make her would be forgotten within moments, the entire conversation for that matter. She picked up the tray, cool against her ribs, and steered toward the door.

"Watch your step, dear!" Miriam called after her.

DOUBT

It was no use trying to sleep. Taking care not to awaken Rowena, David rose from bed in a darkness so complete it seemed some bottomless netherworld. He felt his way to the closet, pulled on a seersucker robe, and stepped out into the low-lit hallway. It was to the library he headed, his refuge in insomnia and heartache.

To David's surprise the lights were on, and inside sat Rashid, thumbing the volume of Neruda he had left bookmarked on the end table earlier that day.

"Awake at this hour?"

"Stuff on my mind," he said and set down the book.

"Yes, well." What could he say to the boy, that brotherhood would prevail and all would be well with the world? They both knew better. "Lionel may have been right, about the incident being random…"

Rashid brushed the remark off. "What's Lebrun doing here?"

"Poking around, he calls it. The mayor is an old friend."

"The mayor might as well be living a fairytale. This speck of nowhere is crawling with fascists."

"I've read in the newspapers about Le Pen and his stooges, but here? It doesn't seem possible."

"What more proof do you need—a burning cross? Your own head on a stake? Look, I never did believe that story about the hot tub."

"No, I didn't suppose you would."

"Someone's got it in for you."

David stepped up to a bookshelf and skimmed titles, hoping to find the cipher that would set his world back on its axis. "What were you doing at the wall," he asked, straining to keep his tone casual, "when they attacked you? Weren't you supposed to be working in the garden?"

"I had seen some wild raspberries growing near the war memorial. I wanted to surprise your mother."

"I didn't notice any berries."

"You've got to have an eye for this sort of thing. The

ones closest to the road had all been picked."

"Of course." In the silence that followed he could not bring himself to look Rashid in the eye.

The boy drew himself up and recited, "I have come back to you from thorny uncertainty—"

"I want you straight as the sword or the road—"

"But you insist on keeping a nook of shadow that I do not want."

"Yes, well. Neruda was not always subtle."

Rashid's hand gravitated to the volume. He said nothing, only sat with his hand resting on the leather cover as if to swear an oath. The cicadas droned, night's heartbeat. "It's so peaceful here, like nothing and no one can mess with your head."

"No place is inviolable. I thought it was enough to be a good neighbor, to live as others live."

"They'll never let you belong, David, any more than they'll let me. Even with your white skin and your *grande maison*. You're a *feuj* and I'm a *beur*—they're just too hypocritical to say it to our faces."

"There *is* kindness in the world." Something he needed to say, the one truth he had clung to through every sleepless night of his adult life.

"Sure, mister."

THE MOOR TAKES LEAVE

"Is that you, Willy?"

"*C'est moi, madame.* Rashid. I didn't mean to wake you."

Where had he come from, this exotic young foreigner with eyes like Omar Sharif? Miriam drew the sheets up to her chin and switched on a lamp. "Who can sleep, dear boy? The rats have come out of the woodwork. But how are you?

I'd have expected them to sink teeth into you by now."

"No chance of that. I've lived with rats all my life."

"Then you know. So wise for your age, and such a noble soul. If only all my subjects were like you."

He brought his hand to his heart, a signature gesture. People from that part of the world were known to emote; it suited them somehow.

"What's that in your breast pocket?"

"Letters. I'll just leave them here, your Highness. You can read them in the morning."

More weary than curious, Miriam watched the young Moor place two envelopes on the mantelpiece. "Nights can be endless. They've given me something to make me sleep, I think. They do things like that, wash your brain with potions. Be strong, dear boy, resist!"

He knelt beside her bed in the manner of a Bedouin courtier and kissed her hand.

She would have liked to stay up talking with him until dawn but felt herself fading, fading... like a ghost about to vanish into thin air. ""Come back in the morning and read me your letter. We'll have tea together, just the two of us. We'll chart a way through this."

AT THE RIVER

Lionel, having slept poorly and awakened before first light, made himself coffee and shuffled out the kitchen door, sipping as he went. He loved mornings, before the phone began ringing and the day's litany of petty claims could rob his peace. The river was at its most alluring then, sunrise's undulating mirror.

As he approached the riverbank, he saw a figure in the distance—male, wiry—drop a small duffle on the ground and make his way along a narrow outcropping of rock to the water's edge. The rocks could be treacherous at that hour, any fool knew, slick with condensation and diesel.

"*Attention!*" he called. "You're out too far."

The figure hesitated but did not retreat. Smelling a suicide, Lionel dropped his coffee mug and raced with arms cranking along the riverbank. It did not take him long to identify the would-be victim.

"Rashid!" Lionel stopped running and paused at a prudent distance to study the boy's face. "Out alone at this hour?"

The boy, exposed and sheepish, inched first in one direction and then the other. "Just taking a walk." Any sudden move might have upset him, sending him headlong into the laughing, indifferent river.

Lionel made eye contact. "*C'est fatal,* this current. We've already had a paddler go overboard this season. Nearly lost him."

"Someone pulled him out?"

"I did," said Lionel, taking a wary step in the boy's direction. "I had a feeling about him."

"Why did he do it?"

"That's what I wanted to know. He told me he was a Turk living in Frankfurt and that life was shit."

The boy faintly nodded. A northerly gusted, making him wince and dance for his footing. "Why didn't the Turk just get it over with over in Germany?"

"My question exactly. He said he didn't want his last memory to be of chrome and contempt—poetic, *non?*"

"Those were his actual words, chrome and contempt?"

The recollection seemed suddenly out of context, the Turk's alliteration contrived. Perhaps Lionel had misunderstood the man; he might as easily have said smog and sauerkraut. "Close enough. The point is there's always something to live for—a morning like this, the breeze coming off the river, a conversation with a friend…" Lionel stretched out a hand. "You do have friends."

"Sure, mister," the boy said.

"Okay, so I wasn't thrilled to have you here, but David loves you like a son."

"Sure, mister."

"*Por Dieu*, let something matter. Life is precious. Don't throw yours away!"

"Honor matters more." The boy looked out over the water, leaned out, set his jaw—Lionel felt his heart crash to the pit of his stomach.

"To a corpse?"

"Without honor life *is* shit. That Turk knew what he was talking about."

Lionel stretched out both his hands. Inching toward solid ground, exhaling, the would-be suicide at last clasped him by a wrist. Not knowing what else to do with the boy's hand, he cradled it.

Rashid broke away and glanced in the direction of the highway, where the village's three crosses stood adorned by plastic flowers and plaster saints.

"Shall I call David?" asked Lionel.

Rashid shook his head, grabbed hold of his battered bag, and like a farm bull testing its tether took a few strides away from him.

Lionel was about to summon the boy back—was he not a delinquent, after all, a danger both to himself and to society? Down the road there would be another river, another synagogue, another provocation to violence. Adolescent zeal, unchecked, was a ticking bomb. And yet the boy looked, not dangerous, but pathetic with his mauled face and bony, sunken shoulders. "Enjoy your walk," the mayor said, stepping aside and watching him steal sadly away.

Lionel in the Dark

Having no one to blame for the heaviness in his heart, which felt at times like a stone and at others like a dagger, Lionel drew the curtains and sat for hours in his armchair.

"Mind if I turn on a light?" Laura, home at last from work.

"A candle would be better."

"I'll get one," she said and felt her way toward the kitchen. "But *Capitaine*, you've left the phone off the hook."

Beautemps could get on without him for one evening.

Laura returned with a lit candelabra, which she set atop the coffee table. "Better, *non?*" Approaching from behind she took him by the shoulders and began to knead. "I ran into David at the charcuterie. He thinks you're avoiding him."

"What does he care?"

"But you're his friend."

"Friend? You'd think I was his worst enemy the way he lambasted me. *Moi,* I was willing to overlook our differences, I accepted him as one of us."

"Of course you did, *Capitaine.*"

"There's no being a friend to—some people."

Her hands went still. "Jews, you mean?"

"Don't go making me out to be some neo-Nazi."

She circled his chair, sat down on the sofa, and curled onto the armrest. "I wouldn't think of it."

"There's nothing I can do about history—the Holocaust, the war with Algeria… I live in the present. Why can't they?"

"David's not like that."

"You didn't hear him."

"Okay, so he was under strain. He bit."

"What does he want from me anyway? I'm just a puny *fonctionaire.* I can't hold off the world. We're under peacetime occupation and it won't end as it did in '45. Who's going to liberate us, José Bové?"

"Astérix."

Lionel laughed in spite of himself, and the candle flames flickered. When the laughter stopped, nostalgia welled up in its place. "I'll do what I can for David, you know that."

"Of course you will, *Capitaine*."

"It may mean we have to put off our vacation. Would you mind that?"

Smiling, she nudged his chair with a stockinged foot. "We've been putting it off for years. Have I ever complained?"

To his daily rounds Lionel added a trip to a private hospital several towns distant, where Madame Fermat lay recuperating from her fall. He had a responsibility toward the old domestic—it had been he, after all, who introduced her to David Crown, he who recommended each to the other. The match may not have been perfect, but neither had had other prospects.

Madame Fermat had been taken by ambulance to the facility and installed at David's expense in a private room. Before making his visit, Lionel had a look at her municipal records and found—who would have believed?—that the housekeeper turned eighty-five within days of the accident. She had no relatives in the *département*, no offspring, only a nephew in Strasbourg, a tradesman of some sort. Her pension was birdseed. Lionel called ahead to see if she needed anything, and she asked him to retrieve a peignoir set and slippers from her apartment and to check on her plants, which were profuse, jungle-like and left little space for her massive pre-war *clapiers* and stacks of chipped china. The neighbor, who held an extra key, stood sentry as he gathered up the few items the patient had requested.

"*C'est grave, n'est-ce pas?*" the gossip intoned, shaking

her layered chins. "They say her hip has splintered."

"Not that bad."

"They say *l' Anglaise* assaulted her, assaulted her and would have killed her. She's crazy, that one. There's a place for people like that."

He opened a drawer at random. "Where might she keep her nightclothes, any idea?"

"Try the chest at the foot of the bed."

The chest held the contents of a vintage trousseau, each article scented with rose water and wrapped in tissue paper. Lionel's gaze fell on a framed photograph lying among the neatly folded garments: Madame Fermat as a bride, her face severe even then yet pretty in its frame of gleaming braids. Her groom beside her, older, already leaning toward stoutness. He smiling, she not.

"Try the bureau," the neighbor prompted.

He followed her lead and soon assembled a small bundle, to which she added a hairbrush, a mirror and a small tube of hand lotion. "A woman has her vanity."

"Have you seen a watering can?"

She shook a finger at him. "That's no job for a busy man. I'll do it."

He thanked her and made for the front door, sidling through the foliage and crockery with the neighbor pinned to his heels. "If you ask me, Madame Fermat ought to press charges at the *préfecture* against the son and mother both. What was he thinking, letting *la folle* run amok like that?"

It was a comment he would hear repeated many times. Madame Fermat, though never popular with her peers, had become an object of pity, the martyred servant of rich foreigners. Details ceased to matter.

Lionel found the *Alsacianne* lying comfortably in the privacy of her room, with a floral arrangement at each elbow and a remote control in her hand. She had been eating chocolate; its telltale remnant darkened the corners of her mouth. A soap opera held her rapt. "So, you've come," she said and reluctantly switched it off.

"*Ça va, madame?* You're looking well."

"First rest I've had in eighty years."

"Staff taking care of you?"

"They're at me day and night. The nurses poke needles into me and the doctors ask questions. One is at their mercy."

"Any visitors?"

"The girl."

"Which girl?"

"*L'Americane.* She told me the *monsieur* had been here earlier, but I was sleeping."

"I've brought your things." He put the parcel on the bed stand, along with a small bouquet of violets purchased from a roadside vendor. "Your neighbor was very helpful. You needn't worry about anything."

"Needn't I? I'm finished." She looked straight ahead as if addressing an invisible jury.

"*Madame*, I must ask you—"

"I'm finished. I'll never work again."

"Are you considering legal action?"

"Against a woman as old as I am? A woman who doesn't even know who she is half the time? Don't be absurd."

A nurse came to the door carrying a blood pressure sleeve. "Did you ring?"

"So many buttons," Madame Fermat said in exasperation. "I can't breathe without setting something off."

Left alone again, they lapsed into a companionable silence.

"Well, I suppose I should be going."

"You'll come again?"

"Yes, certainly."

"It was Durand, you know. He's one of Le Pen's."

Lionel felt the breath catch in his throat. "How can you be sure?"

"The paint. He bought it to brighten-up that old jalopy of his but decided against it. It was undignified, making something that old stand out like a canary. So, he put it to more fitting use."

"But why the Crowns?"

"That's what I said to him, why the *monsieur*? He pays you well. But that's what those people do, buy their way into a place."

"Where is Durand now?"

"In the garden, I suppose. He looks after those plants like a priest after souls."

"Get some rest," he said mechanically, already halfway to the door.

"Strange people, the Crowns." She gave an indulgent little cluck. "Stomachs like cattle."

"If there's anything you need—"

"That's what the American said, whatever I need."

"They'll do right by you," Lionel assured her.

She swatted the remark away as if it were a cobweb. "I depend on no one. If this hip doesn't mend, I myself will call the glue factory to come get me."

DAVID TAKES COURAGE

Without the wooden serenade of Madame Fermat's clogs, life in the *Vie Dorée* lost its rhythm. For hours at a stretch there was no sound at all. When at last the doorbell rang, it set David's heart heaving.

On the doorstep, backlit, stood Laura Olivier, a briefcase gently swinging at her side. "*Salut*, David. *Ça va*, *chéri?* You look like *ze espace cadette.*"

"Come in, please." They kissed cheeks and he led her across the foyer into the parlor. "Sit. Let me get you something—tea, coffee?"

She perched rather than sat on a straight-backed chair and waved his offer away with an easy grace. "I can't stay long. Lionel told me what happened."

No doubt the entire village knew by then.

"How is your mother?"

"Quiet—too quiet, perhaps. She doesn't leave her bed."

"Might she want to counsel with someone, a rabbi?"

"I don't know. I don't know how her mind works anymore. She's not religious." Though Laura's manner suggested nothing but solicitude, he felt obliged to defend Miriam. "She would never intentionally hurt anyone."

"Of course not."

"She was, in her way, fond of Madame Fermat."

"Madame Fermat is not known for inspiring affection. She's a decent woman and a lonely one, I suspect. We'll see that she's looked after. And you, *mon pauvre*, left without a housekeeper. *Tenez.*" She handed him a business card. "A friend's agency. Temporary help."

"Thank you, Laura. Thank you very much indeed."

She rose and smoothed back her pinned chignon. "Call me on my mobile if you need anything."

"I don't suppose Lionel would welcome a call?"

"Perhaps not, *chéri.* Not yet."

"How is he?"

She gestured a *comme-ci comme-ca.* "Sulking. People think because Lionel is in politics that he has *ze theeck* skin, but he's a soft man. He bruises easily."

"I was harsh."

"*C'est normal.* You had a shock."

"Mother had a worse one. If you had seen her face…

what terror she had to have been holding inside."

"Terror?"

"She was lucky, her grandfather chose to immigrate to England, but her aunts, uncles, cousins—gone. For years she searched the lists. What's to stop it all happening again, Drancy, Auschwitz?"

"We mustn't let it," she said with sudden passion, "we won't let it."

"Brave new world."

"Not so brave, *chèri*, just sobered." Having fulfilled her mission, she lifted her briefcase from the floor and drew David to his feet. "Let Lionel marinate a few days, then drop by. Don't wait too long."

He nodded.

She walked briskly to the foyer and he followed, pausing there to repeat their cheek-kissing ritual. "*Bon courage*," she said in parting.

"Will do," David assured her and closed the door. He wandered in and out of the downstairs rooms, heartsick and wanting to speak with someone, someone wiser than he. Once, that someone had been Miriam. He headed to the kitchen and heaped a breakfast tray with toast and marmalade, a pot of tea, a cut rose. Balancing the tray on his shoulder, he ascended the marble stairs two-at-a-time, strode the length of the corridor, and knocked lightly at his mother's door.

"Is that you, Willy?" he heard her call.

He stepped into the room with its drawn curtains and clustered pill bottles. "Sleep well, Mum?"

"Our young Moor has decamped," Miriam said in a broken voice and began to sob.

David set down the tray, curled beside her on the canopy bed, and clumsily patted her hand. "Rashid, gone? Are you certain?"

"He left these letters—one for you, one for me." She handed him an envelope monogrammed with his own initials and tucked the other beneath her pillow. "I checked the green room, not a trace of him."

David turned the letter over in his hands.

"Aren't you going to open it?"

"I need a moment." David recalled his last conversation with the boy, not what was said but the vague suspicions that embittered each word.

"That dear, dear boy... where will he go? It's me, isn't it? Something is off up here." She pointed to her forehead, which had furrowed in the manner of a cat's cradle.

"Misunderstandings, Mum. Things will come right."

Miriam tilted sideways into his arms and nestled there like a child. "He cared for us in his way. He counted on us. Could we have done better, Davey, loved him better?"

THE ENEMY

Habibi:

I wouldn't have minded the looks and whispers, Madame Fermat's tantrums, Durand's put-downs... I expect that shit from *them*. But you, David, even you had your doubts about me. All it took was a reminder, a few swastikas, and I became the enemy.

It is human to doubt—that's not why I'm leaving. I'm leaving because they hate you more when I'm around. They hate seeing some *mufti* Jew playing Moses to a juvenile terrorist from the *banlieues*—did you think you'd get away with it?

I've done some growing up in this castle of yours and am ready to admit that what I did at the synagogue was a mistake. I have thanked God every day that no one was hurt. You have no idea what it has cost me to look you in the eye.

There's just one thing I wish I could ask you: Was this ever personal? You always did the right thing, always stood up for me, but never once embraced me or called me *copain*.

And maybe we were both naïve, you for thinking you could save me, and I for wanting to be something more than a cause.

I am leaving behind your poetry books. Pretty words won't help me where I'm going.

Rashid

Rescue Mission

The books were what hurt the most, that the boy would abandon the one thing that had lifted him, mind and spirit, above the squalid circumstances of his life, that he would go off—where, David hadn't a clue—with nothing but a few euro and a change of clothes. What would David have given at that moment to embrace the boy? Not pausing to think, he swiped his car keys from the foyer table, tore down the winding driveway in his estate car, and headed for the city.

As he drove, he rehearsed what he would say to Rashid were he to find him, but nothing sounded right. He wanted only to bring the boy home and sit with him in the library skimming volumes of Eliot and Lawrence. Without poetry the boy's future could only be bleak, a stifling cell with no conduit to truth or beauty.

David drew up to Paradise and parked. He strode through the vestibule, mounted the narrow stairs, and knocked at the peeling door of 666.

"*Qui est là?*" called someone inside.

"Rashid?"

The door jarred open and out stepped Emile, unshaven, bare-chested. "You, here?" He circled vulture-like.

"You got no business here."

"I'm looking for Rashid."

"I thought he was with you?"

"He was—until this morning."

"I'm just glad he had the sense not to come here." He started to re-enter the flat, but turned back to gloat, "So, Rashid told you where to get off. He couldn't be bought."

"It wasn't like that."

"You saying I don't know my own brother? Watch it, mister, you're on my turf now." He brushed past David, descended the stairs (a line of tattoos extended from the nape of his neck to the waistband of his sweatpants), and leaned in the doorway. "However it was, Rashid's on the street somewhere. Nice work. Lot of good all your meddling has done him."

"Okay, so I've made some mistakes, but reaching out to your brother wasn't one of them. I'm prepared to become his legal guardian, to look after him while he gets an education."

Emile veered as if to strike a blow. "You some sort of *perv*, mister?"

"No, just someone who wants to see a great kid get a break. If you want to hate me for that, go right ahead."

"Did you screw my mother?"

"Certainly not!"

"The only *mec* in France who didn't." The menace drained from his stance, leaving him just another unhappy teenager enduring adolescence. "My old man finally threw her out."

"I'm sorry."

"What do you got to be sorry about? You, with your mansion and bling life."

"If you should hear from Rashid—"

"He has your number." A pair of girls with hula-hoops sidled, giggling, through the door. Emile gave the less coordinated of the two a hand.

"You must have some idea where he would go?"

"Somewhere with work—not that he'll get any. Somewhere he can blend in." Emile started up the stairwell. "If you should find my brother," he said in a voice drained of hope, "tell him to stay the hell away from this place. Tell him… hell, what do I know?"

David stepped out into high noon. Most of the teenagers had sought shade under the scant few trees near the dumpsters, leaving the two hula-hoopers free to wriggle and contort up and down the length of the parking lot.

He found his Volvo where he had left it—minus its four Michelin tires. He removed a note, scrawled in pencil on the inside of a take-out bag, from underneath the windshield wiper: "Nice wheels, *mec*."

In the distance, laughter. David, not knowing what else to do, got into the car and gazed about in all directions. Were the thieves still hovering, waiting to take his Rolex, his wallet, the gold fillings from his teeth? Might he be safer with Emile? Bracing for a dressing-down, he called the one person who would know what to do.

"Lebrun? Crown here. May I trouble you to call me a taxicab? Little trouble with the Volvo."

"Where are you?" the lieutenant asked.

"Outside the Hamadi residence—what's it called?"

"You out of your freaking mind, Crown?" Lebrun had to have been screaming into the mouthpiece. "Leave the car, leave everything, and get the hell out of there. Walk and keep walking until you find a public place—a store, a restaurant— that isn't crawling with Arabs."

"No one is being overtly hostile. I just need a ride."

"You've got no idea. Walk! Find someplace on a major thoroughfare, visible, well-lit."

"All right. I'll call you when I get there."

"No, you won't. You'll stay on this phone with me. I'm heading your way right now." David heard the familiar roar of Lebrun's Triumph followed by the wail of a siren. "Now walk, Crown, keep your fancy head down and walk…"

How It Starts

That evening Lionel paid a call on the gardener, Durand, whose home lay on the village's fringe between a pig farm and the old schoolhouse (recently converted to a yoga studio). Squat, square and unadorned, the house echoed its owner's basic appearance, the only difference being its majestic chimney, where a lone stork had come to nest.

A light was on and through the uncurtained window Lionel could see Durand, dozing in front of a small-screened television set. Durand's companion, an ill-tempered bulldog rescued from the pound, began to bark. Durand roused, switched-off the TV, and tramped to the door.

"What do you want?" the old man said through the keyhole.

"Come out here. We need to talk."

The door opened and the gardener stood on the threshold with arms tightly crossed.

"I know what you did, Durand. What's gotten into you, anyway—defacing public property, assaulting a boy, inciting racial hatred?" The bulldog lunged for his heel and nipped it, bringing the hint of a smile to its master's face.

"Come off it, Olivier. You don't like immigrants any more than I do. You see what they've done to our cities. Is that what you want for Beautemps?"

"Peaceful coexistence is what I want. The rule of law is what I aim to uphold."

"This is how it starts: First it's one Jew, one Arab; next it will be their families, their extended families, their communities... This is *our* country. It's up to us to draw the line."

Lionel mustered authority. "I could have you put away for this."

"Go ahead. My cronies in the National Front will have a heyday and you can forget about ever holding public office again."

"Goddam it, Durand, you're old enough to be my grandfather."

"What of it?"

"You've lived through two world wars." The horror of which Lionel could only imagine from grisly images of mutilated corpses and cities laid waste. "Haven't you had enough hell on earth?"

"You're like all the rest of them, spouting homilies while France is overrun by aliens. Soon we won't recognize our own country. I want to die in my *pays* among people I know. Can't a man die in peace?"

"Then keep your politics for the voting booth—and your hunting rifle for the hunt. Your license is due for renewal, by the way."

"I suppose you've raised the fees again?" A look of umbrage overspread the gardener's weathered mug. "And *moi* without a job."

"Monsieur Crown doesn't know. You're still his gardener. This stays between us, *d'accord?*"

Durand assented with an upward nod. "I've got nothing against Crown, you know. It's a matter of principle."

"I don't want to hear any more about your stinking principles and your stinking politics. My friends in the ministry would love to make an example of a bigot like you. One word from me and you're out of a job and in the clinker."

The dog reappeared, dragging a desiccated mouse by

the tail. Durand nudged it away with the reinforced toe of his work boot.

"We never thought you'd come back. It broke your father's heart, you at sea and the land going to seed. Yet here you are, lording it over the rest of us."

"What you think of me is immaterial. For as long as I hold this miserable office, Beautemps will be a place where no law-abiding person need fear for his safety. Tell your cronies that."

DAVID WRESTLES WITH GOD

From the time David first learned to read, whenever confusion threatened to overwhelm him or adversity to break his spirit, he had found succor, not at a place of worship, but in the stacks of a library. It was there that he sought love, and there he returned in the aftermath of Rashid's departure.

He drifted though the aisles unhurried, pausing to open books at random and read the first sentence that caught his eye. An hour later, glutted and needing to ruminate, he walked toward an empty chair. For cover he pulled a book from a nearby shelf and held it, unopened, on his lap. A bearded man in an embroidered gauze shirt sat down next to him. Normally, David would not have noticed him, but as he read he laughed softly, rocked in his seat. David cast sideways glances at him, wondering at his merriment. Sensing David's interest the stranger cocked his head.

"*Je vous dérange, monsieur?*" he asked in a tone of apology.

"Not at all."

A small knitted yamulke peeked out from beneath his unruly hair, which unlike David's own impressed with its abundance. "Rabelais," he volunteered, turning the cover of the tome toward him. "I don't usually read novels but my daughter says it's time I broaden my horizons. *Et vous?*"

"I read anything I can lay hands on."

"A thinker," he said approvingly. David expected him to go back to his book, but instead he angled his chair toward him and asked, "What are you reading now?"

David took the book from his lap and scanned its title for the first time: *Secrets de la Cuisine Minceur.*

"Surely you are not on a diet?"

"No, no." He thrust the book aside.

"You are English? I can always tell an Englishman; he speaks without moving his lips." Again the low infectious laugh. "But we've met, *non?* I never forget a face."

"Unlikely. I live some distance from here."

Thinking aloud, the stranger finger-combed his beard. "The filling station, the hypermarket, the cinema…?"

"The synagogue," David heard himself whisper.

The fluorescent lights flared, tingeing the rabbi's face a torrid orange. Petrol fumes, smoke, and the books a maelstrom of ashes rising. Another instant and the windows would shatter—

"Are you all right?" He placed an ink-stained hand upon David's shoulder.

"I am, now."

He retracted his hand and sat back, resting his palms on a softly rounded paunch. "I remember. You took the Torah from my arms, took it without hesitation. How it must have pained you!"

"It was a comfort. The pain came after."

"I know."

"The fire, inside me it's still smoldering."

"We're wrestlers with God," the rabbi said lowering his voice, matching its rhythm to the silent pounding of his fist against the chair leg. "We don't submit."

"We?"

"We Jews. You are Jewish, aren't you?" David hesitated and he went on, "What happened at the synagogue, it's not something you get over from one day to the next." A shadow crept across his broad cheeks. "Please forgive me, Monsieur?"

"Crown. David Crown."

The rabbi gave an abbreviated bow. "Aaron Baumander, *a votre disposition.*

David felt his eyes moisten. "The boys who threw the petrol bombs, I've met them."

"A *mitzvah,* a good deed. I had been meaning to make contact myself, but with the congregation so distraught..." The rabbi leaned intently forward. "Tell me more."

"They think Jews are responsible for their lot in life, that it is we who keep them down. What would you say to them, rabbi?"

"Dogma is less useful than cow dung."

David had heard the adage. "Buber? Spinoza?"

"Mao Zedong." Baumander gave an impish wink. "My point being, it's too late for words. Sometimes individuals must act and then wait for society to catch up."

"The older one wants nothing to do with me. The younger has such potential but is so terribly vulnerable. I'd do anything to protect him, if only I knew how."

"Every one of us is vulnerable. I am a rabbi and a rabbi has license, not because he is wise but because he is at war with ignorance. There's an expression in the Torah, 'as a man thinketh in his heart.' People nowadays think with their heads only—you have noticed, *non?* To them the heart is nothing but a pump."

David couldn't deny this.

"Every day there are fewer of us, more of them. It's not religion that separates us; it's what we dare to feel, how much we're willing to endure in order to keep our hearts whole. Tell your young man that."

"One day I will."

"Thanks be to God, we're alive, the synagogue was spared; another few weeks and the renovation will be complete. You must come spend a Sabbath with us."

"Yes, of course," David said without conviction.

The rabbi inclined toward him, his gaze more nuanced at close range. "I take it you have broken with the tribe? *Tant pis.* No ready answers for you, no community. But *famille*—surely you have family?" David nodded, and the rabbi looked relieved. "What brought you to the synagogue that day?"

"If I knew… something more than idle curiosity—a pang of remorse? A sort of echo…"

"A person needs a story."

"You've lost me, rabbi."

"The Torah, the story of our tenancy upon this earth. Why do people come to synagogue? To take their place in the story—to be immortal."

"And the firebombing?"

"A mere footnote."

David laughed then, laughed until his sides ached and tears trickled down his cheeks. Mirth drained abruptly from the cackle leaving it a hiccupping dirge. Struggling to contain himself, he drew out a handkerchief.

"But I have upset you."

"No. It's a bit much to take in, that's all." David lowered his eyes, fearing another spill.

"You will go home soon?"

"I thought I had built myself a home."

The rabbi's hand cupped the scruff of David's neck and drew him forward until they were head-to-head, locked in a combat of love. David could have breathed his breath. "Your roots are longer than you know, David Crown, longer than you know."

OLD SCORES

Lionel arrived home to find Lebrun lounging in his favorite armchair, drinking the brandy he reserved for wedding toasts and visiting dignitaries.

"I let myself in," the lieutenant said and went on drinking.

Lionel set down his car keys and changed into his boating shoes. "Let's get out of here."

"What for?" Lebrun arched into a yawn, thrusting out his beefy chest. "Have the deadly paint-can duo struck again?"

Lionel ignored the remark, pulled on his yachting cap, and went outside. Lebrun, helmet in hand, followed.

"Let's take the *moto*," said the lieutenant. "I hate to walk."

"*D'accord*, but just to the river."

They mounted and breezed through the village, bypassing the thinning throng of tourists, and arrived at Lionel's shack as a misty dusk settled over the water.

"How about a paddle, for old time's sake?"

They launched the *Caribbean Caprice* and were soon mid-river, carried by a navigable, if assertive, current. The sun began its slow melt over the hills; the treetops filled with starts.

Lebrun commandeered the oars. "You never could row worth a rat's ass."

Lionel, having learned to pick his fights, let the remark pass. "We never much liked each other, Lebrun, but I've always respected you."

"Likewise, but why the sudden tribute?"

"Because I want you to leave Beautemps and not come back." Lebrun stopped rowing.

"I know, I know... it was I who asked you here. A moment

of weakness."

"You've done nothing but jerk me around."

"*C'est vrai*, I've handled things clumsily, but consider the circumstances. I'm a village mayor not the *Ministre de l'Intérieur*."

"And I'm a police lieutenant," spat Lebrun, his face livid and beading with sweat, "not some pussy you can order about."

"You don't change. You're the same snot-nose you were in the Navy, always having to show how tough you are. That's not how things are done in Beautemps."

"You conniving *bouffon!* I smell a cover-up. If it's not the kid, it's a local, isn't it?" He reached over and smacked Lionel's cheek, as if to incite a duel. The boat took on water. "Isn't it?"

"That's no longer your concern. You've been recalled to your unit, effective immediately."

Barely were the words out when Lebrun rammed an oar into Lionel's solar plexus, knocking him backwards. "How can you expect people to respect the law if the mayor himself doesn't?"

Clutching his ribs, Lionel strained upright. "*Calme-toi, por dieu.*"

"*Du calme, Du calme...*" Lebrun reared back and struck a second blow, a sidewinder, sending Lionel overboard.

Spitting out sediment he surfaced, caught his breath, and reached out for a handhold. "*Zut!* This water is ice cold."

"Little cold water never hurt anyone." Wielding the oar like a pestle the cop butted Lionel from the side of the boat. "You've gone soft, lost your mettle."

Lionel, at ease on water, less at ease *in* it, felt his limbs go numb. "That's enough joking around. Let me back in the boat."

"*Let me back in the boat,*" Lebrun parroted and peeling off his motorcycle jacket leapt overboard. "You always were a pussy."

"And you a sadist and a bully—not to mention a womanizer. You think I don't know that you propositioned Laura?"

"Oh that... I'd had a few drinks."

"How dare you! You come anywhere near my wife and I'll—" Lionel grabbed his old chum by the hair and dunked him, holding his head underwater for the count.

"That was almost thirty years ago," Lebrun sputtered, gasping for breath. "You weren't even married."

"She has always been a part of my soul, but that means nothing to a dickhead like you. You macho types give the rest of us a bad name. You make me ashamed to be a man."

"You, a man? I don't know whether to laugh or to wring your girly little gizzard." Lebrun lunged through the froth and applying a scissor-lock dragged Lionel down into the drink.

Through the darkness and slime Lionel felt some immense, distant voice beckon, whether life or death he couldn't have said, but peace enveloped him like a mother's embrace. Lebrun, his face obscured by air bubbles, flipped him the finger and let go. Weightless, wielding, he floated to the surface, followed by his assailant, the two men blue and breathless with cold. "You'll get us both killed, and for what? The kid has decamped. David Crown has shut himself away like King Tut in his tomb. There's nothing for you here."

"This village of yours is going to pot, Olivier, but still the same air of superiority."

"Superiority? If you knew... Every day I feel less in control of my life, powerless to shape the future. My own children don't want to come back to this village. What good am I to anyone?"

"*Merde.* Spare us both the pity party and get back in the boat." Lebrun, his teeth audibly chattering, held the boat stable while Lionel climbed aboard.

Lionel held out a hand for Lebrun, who refused it and hoisted himself over the edge like a moribund sea porpoise. The mayor, oddly exalted, began to row. Autumn was in the air. "You had better dry off, *mon vieux.* I've got a bottle of brandy back at the kiosk."

VILLAGE HERO

There is the matter of Swijdendorp's poachers still to tell. For months their pilfering plagued the Dutch farmer, until it seemed they were consuming him rather than his crop. Little remained of his person but angles.

With the *Vie Dorée* in disorder David continued his nocturnal patrolling. To walk in starlight through the open fields cleared his mind. Lionel no longer joined him. He walked alone training his eyes on the tree trunks, listening, alert to every sigh of the wind, to the river's trills and murmurs. Any moment the poachers might lurch into his path. The farmer had warned David they would be armed and tried to force a rifle on him, but he had never touched a gun let alone fired one. The carving knife tucked in his belt would have to do.

For seven nights David ranged over Swijdendorp's holding, encountering nothing but the occasional hare or fox. The farmer had set traps. David kept his eyes on the ground. To stay awake he recited poems learned in childhood: *The owl and the pussycat went to sea in a beautiful pea-green boat...Is there anybody there? said the traveller, knocking on the moonlit door...* His repertoire wouldn't last the night. *I wandered lonely as a cloud...*

Above his recitation a piercing shriek of pain.

He veered toward the cry, straining his eyes in the semi-darkness for a source that might have been human, animal, chimera... not knowing what he was looking for. His torch cast only a short beam of light. He switched it off. Voices. Steering in their direction he detected two figures, men like himself. With his right hand poised on the hilt of his weapon, he raced toward them.

The intruders didn't run away, and as David drew near, he understood why. One of them, snared by a trap, hung upside-down from his wrenched ankle. Curses poured from him. His companion, having nothing with which to sever the cord that bound him, could only pull at the leg. As David drew up, the free man turned to him with his palms open; though tall and burly, he seemed to pose no threat.

"You, Russ?"

"Jeez," said the American, "am I glad to see you."

"Cut me down, sod it," the trapped man moaned. Cecil Rhodes. Rhodes, dangling like a hog carcass.

Griffith, obviously tipsy yet glib, mindful of his role, glanced toward his companion. "You all right, pal?" Then to David, "Just picking a couple of truffles for our Sunday omelet."

"Bloody ankle wrenched, bladder about to burst..."

"Cut him down—will you, Crown?—and we'll be on our way."

"Like hell you will."

Griffith clapped him on the arm. "Be a sport. Swijdendorp hasn't seen us."

"But I have."

"You're making too much of this. It was a prank. A couple of truffles..."

"It's a man's livelihood. Have you any idea what it is to work for a living?"

"Not really and you're hardly the fellow to teach me."

David turned on the torch and shone it upwards. "Over here, Arjen!" he called at full volume. "I've got your poachers."

"You're a stupid arse, Crown."

"If you weren't trussed up like a pig, Rhodes, I'd punch your pretty face." Shining his flashlight David called again. "Over here!"

A man strode up but it was not the farmer. Lionel, a windbreaker only partially covering his striped pajamas, rubbed his eyes. "Monsieur Griffith? Monsieur Rhodes? I heard shouting."

David had not seen Lionel since their confrontation at the war memorial. Despite his attire and bed-tousled hair, the mayor conducted himself with authority. Their eyes did not meet.

In an instant Arjen appeared, wielding a pitchfork. "Christ," he said and shone his flashlight in Rhodes' face. "This your idea of a joke? Ten years, ten years I've worked this soil."

"Screw you. Cut me down."

David took the kitchen knife from his belt and slashed the cord. Rhodes crumpled to the ground with a grunt.

Griffith, stifling a smile, sidled up to the injured thief. "Use a hand, pal?"

"Piss off." Rhodes righted himself and hobbled away on his one good leg.

"I'd better look after him," said Griffith, setting off at a trot.

Lionel called out, "You'll be hearing from the gendarmes."

The American doubled back. "Really, guys, couldn't we just settle up among ourselves?" Billfold in hand, he turned toward the farmer.

"Put it away, Griffith," David told him, "this is no gambling debt."

Rhodes, having not gotten far, spat in their direction. "You've crippled me, miserable pack of killjoys. Screw you, Crown. Screw you all!"

When David arrived home Miriam was awake, prowling the hallways in her underclothes. "Where have you been?" she asked, folding her hands beneath a white brassiere that reached to her waist.

"Swijdendorp's," David said and averted his eyes.

Evincing no shame, she rested a hand on her nylon half-slip and with the other tapped at his ribs. "That's where Rowena goes, isn't it? To that farm across the way."

He found it hard to take a next breath.

"Have I said something I oughtn't?"

"Let me bring you a robe, Mum."

She looked down at herself with a grimace. "On the bed. The pink one." Once she had pulled on the robe and knotted its sash, he walked her back down the passage to her bedroom. A lamp remained lit beside her vanity table. She sat down before the mirror and gazed back at him in the glass. "Your sweetheart has strayed, dear boy."

As David lay in bed that night stealing glances at Rowena asleep with her legs askew and one pink nipple exposed above her cotton chemise, desire hardened into suspicion. He drew aside the sheet and studied her face, her throat, the cleft between her breasts. He inched up her nightie. She was no less beautiful for having deceived him. Turning away, he fell into the iron vise of sleep.

News of the poachers' disgrace buzzed through Beautemps like a chainsaw. For the remainder of the season Rhodes and Griffith, their reputations cut to ribbons, made themselves scarce. Their wives took to wearing wide-brimmed hats. To David's embarrassment much was made of his part in apprehending the hapless duo. French neighbors accosted him in the street with V-signs and kisses, as if he'd liberated the village rather than spared it the loss of a few clods of fungus. Rowena returned from the charcuterie with a long-stemmed rose jutting from her shopping sack, compliments of the proprietor.

"People are talking as if you'd saved a national treasure. You're the village hero."

"It's your hero I had hoped to be."

"Didn't that sort of thing go out with John Wayne?"

Having been dubbed a re-run, he snatched up the groceries and walked them to the pantry.

"*Aoh deah*, I've offended you again. Look, heroism just isn't something I've come across in real life."

"Perhaps I should have left you to your books."

"You *are* offended. Look, we're both on edge right now. Let's not argue."

"I've heard about your visits to Swijdendorp."

She met his gaze. "So, that's it. And you think—"

"I don't think anything."

"Swijdendorp, the lady killer. Surely you don't think—"

"I don't think anything and I'm not asking."

"Dammit, you have a right to know!" She backhanded a tub of butter, sending it skittering along the countertop. "There's nothing between me and Swijdendorp. It's a case of two social outcasts thrown together by default. We're a couple of freaks, for chrissake."

"Don't talk like that. Please."

"I've not exactly been a hit with the village clique."

"To your credit."

She plunged the rose, already swooning, into a glass of water. "It's all gone so wrong."

"Not entirely." David would have taken her in his arms but the signals weren't clear. Her nearness was like a purring, it asked to be petted, but her eyes said *don't*. "Are you off of me?"

"Off of you, no. Just off." And for once she looked it, her expression filmy and faded like a painting needing restoration. "I suppose I'd better leave, huh?"

"Over Swijdendorp?" He almost laughed. "By no means."

"We were happy once, weren't we?"

"We'll be happy again."

She seemed to mull this. "So, we pull up stakes and start over?"

"I don't want to leave the *Vie Dorée*. What if Rashid were to come back and find us gone?"

"Look, I'm fond of the kid too, but it's your mother we need to think about now. When did she last leave her room? She can't stay here, not after what's happened."

No tidy solution leapt to mind, only questions. "Where does that leave us, you and I?"

"When you have a concrete proposal, let's talk."

By the time David had assessed their options and pieced together a future of modest if noble aims, she was no longer in a mood to talk. Wanderlust had spun her around like a wheel of fortune. Three days later, she was gone.

ROWENA'S SECRET

The call came as Rowena was packing the last of her things. She didn't recognize the muffled male voice at first.

"Are you all right?" Barely a whisper but the accent was Swijdendorp's, the tone earthy and dry.

"You shouldn't be calling me here," she chided and felt the heat rise to her head.

"Don't worry, I won't crack. I'll never tell."

"I know you won't," she said, unconvinced. The need to confess was stronger than the will to keep silent, any Catholic knew.

"I was thinking of shooting the dogs."

"Don't."

"I'll never crack."

Numb, null, she switched off. Uttered at the edge of an abyss, words were such hollow things.

A LAST GAME OF CHESS

When finally David came to Lionel, as Lionel knew he would, his manner held no animosity; to the contrary it evinced nothing but remorse. *Tant pis*. He might have spared himself the self-flagellation. The Frenchman had forgiven him long ago.

"I was passing by…"

"*Ça va*, David?" Lionel motioned him inside and onto the sofa as he had dozens of times before, his way of saying nothing had changed, though this was not strictly true. Each of them had glimpsed in the other a mirror image of his own mulishness. "I don't suppose you've heard from Rashid?"

He hadn't.

"Lebrun will keep an eye out for him. The boy will turn up."

"It was Durand, wasn't it?" said David in a tightly contained voice. "Rashid was telling the truth."

"So, you know. You know and yet you've kept the old diehard on."

"The man's a relic, afraid of change."

"I wanted to tell you, wanted a friend with whom to puzzle it all out."

"I don't care a rat's arse about Durand, but I hate to think of Rashid back on the streets alone or worse, in bad company."

Would David never get that boy out of his mind? Lionel himself couldn't, and yet it seemed prudent to change the subject, to speak of the few things over which they still had a modicum of control. "Prison would kill Durand. His insides were battered pretty badly during the war—not that that absolves him."

"And his accomplice?"

"There's a bunch of old-timers who have gone over to Le Pen, a last stand of sorts. They consider themselves patriots. It wouldn't have occurred to me to take them seriously until—how blind I was!"

"No blinder than I, my friend."

"David, David… you came here with such dreams. Even if Beautemps had been heaven itself, we couldn't have lived up to your ideals. Your *vie dorée* was always in peril. I should have warned you; I tried to. Forgive me."

"There's nothing to forgive."

Lionel took a deep breath and felt the knot of dread he had been carrying in his throat slacken and dissolve. "Laura has been keeping something for you." He rifled through a cupboard until his hands seized on the desired object: a finger-sized piece of worked metal. "*Voila!* Some sort of talisman, *non?*"

"It's called a mezuzah. Jews—some Jews—hang them on the doorpost. Must be very old."

"Laura found it in her *pays* near her parents' home. Apparently, there was once a Jewish quarter there. Items turn up now and again. We send them to the *Musée de la Préfecture*." David passed the object back to Lionel. "Take it. No use its gathering dust in some museum."

"What could it mean?" the Englishman murmured, turning it over and over in his hands.

Hoping to rouse him, Lionel invited him to a pastis.

"Another time perhaps." At last he pocketed the charm.

"Game of chess?"

"A last game. I'm putting the house on the market."

"You'll have no trouble renting it."

"The house is for sale, Lionel."

Lionel could feel his dark mood creep back. "But you've barely completed the renovation…" David's silence left no space for revisions, but he couldn't help suggesting, "Why not wait for springtime? I hear it's raining like the end of days up north."

The Englishman shrugged and set his jaw. "I don't think I shall mind the weather this year."

Parting Shots

A dream abandoned, sold for scrap—is this what David's story amounted to in the end?
His final days in Beautemps were taken up with arrangements. Once Rowena had left his bed, there remained only a checklist: settle Madame Fermat, sell the house, service the Volvo… He wanted it over quickly, before another honeyed sunrise or chorus of cuckoos could tempt him to stay. He wanted it over so the forgetting could begin.

Only after he had checked off the last item, scoured every closet, emptied every drawer, did he pass by the garage and recall with a twinge the matched gargoyles, smothered in wrapping paper and plastic sheeting and shunted like naughty children into a corner. He couldn't just leave them there, neither had he any intention of shipping them north. There was only one solution. Donning a dust mask, he gave them a thorough cleaning, hefted them into the back of his estate car, and drove down the driveway to *Maison Joyeuse.*

The front gate stood ajar. Wrestling with one at a time, David half carried half dragged the dozing monks up the path to Hedy's doorstep. Dodging their lidded stares he searched for a bell or buzzer but found instead a brass gong and mallet. It seemed more straightforward to knock. Hedy didn't answer at once. Chastened, he struck the gong and waited.

"If that's you, Cecil," she called, "get stuffed!"

He turned, tripping over the monks, and was about to retrace his steps when Hedy swung wide the door and started forward, poised to strike a blow. "Wrong," she said and shrank back against the doorframe. "What can I do for you, Mr. Crown? I suppose you'll want to redecorate. I've heard about the departure of the fair Rowena. A little change of ambience can do wonders. *Ah*, I know just the thing: hemp. It's all the rage and so green."

"Thank you, but that's not why I've come. Actually—"

She turned and walked back into the house. When he didn't follow, she walked out again, said, "Aren't you coming?" and led him inside by a shirtsleeve. "Close the door."

"I would have called but—"

"I've missed you, admittedly, but I do have my pride. The way men grovel and fall before youth! It's pathetic, despicable, the shallowness of it. I wouldn't have expected it in you, but I rather overestimated you. In many ways."

"You don't look at all well, Hedy." David's eye fell on a silver flask jutting from the patch pocket of her roomy sundress. "May I get you something?"

"I'm quite well. Quite. We in Beautemps enjoy a disproportionate grace, deserved or not. But you look rather stricken, Mr. Crown. Have I tweaked something?"

"Cecil expected back?"

"Oh him… But I haven't offered you anything—wine, vodka? At times like these, sobriety is the worst thing. *Pas normal, verboten,* just plain stupid, in fact." She raised the flask as if to propose a toast.

"Shall I call Deirdre? I need to be going."

"Always running off—afraid of me?" She clasped him by the placket of his shirt and pulled him flush against her.

There seemed to be no bones beneath her flesh, she was soft everywhere, an aggregation of mounds. Not knowing how else to restrain her, he took her hands. "But what a pussycat you are, even now, without that little witch standing guard. I couldn't stand her, you know. Pseudo-intellectual, self-righteous. Could have told you months ago she'd run off, but to cuckold you like that. Come on, have a drink. Get comfy."

"Hedy, I'm leaving. I've come to say goodbye."

"Not goodbye, darling. Toodaloo, until next season."

"Mother and I won't be back."

"You're a goddam fool not to take advantage of the situation. I may not be in the first bloom of youth, but I'm told my attributes have held up pretty well. Pretty damn well. Perhaps it's yours that haven't—of course, why didn't I think of it? Pity that. Well, do kiss me at least." She rose on tiptoe and collapsed against him, leaving him no choice but to buoy her up with his arms.

"We mustn't."

She took back her weight and, pouting, said, "You don't like me, why?"

"Let me call Deirdre."

"I don't want Deirdre. I don't want anyone." She walked heavily toward a portable bar.

"Let me make you a cup of tea."

"Why couldn't you like me? Why can't you? Hell, don't answer that—don't answer and don't try and be kind." She took a bottle, an empty, and dashed it to the floor. "You goddam fool."

There seemed no point in lingering.

"I oughtn't have done that," she scolded herself and prodded the shards with her sole.

Keeping her in his sights, he edged toward the door.

"Go then," she said, trailing at a distance.

Only at the doorstep did he remember the mission that had brought him. "The gargoyles, Hedy, I'd like you to have them."

"I'm off gargoyles just now. Goodbye, David."

LIONEL TAKES TWO ASPIRIN

The foreign community began its annual migration north, an orderly and methodical exodus—pools emptied, water pipes bled, doors padlocked, the property manager on hand to take possession of a set of keys. There were few goodbyes as their Range Rovers and Jaguars hauled away the sheepdogs and bric-a-brac, the *foie gras* and crates of local wine. They would be back soon enough.

Lionel put the canoe business on winter hours, checked his sweaters for moth holes, brought in the firewood. Although the weather remained warm, the days' margins had contracted; mornings began in half-light. The cranes wheeled away.

As the village's population dwindled so did Lionel's troubles. Blissful as an escapee he went fishing, but his relief proved premature. Deirdre Griffith waited on his doorstep pacing in peckish little box steps. As he admitted her she said, "I missed you at the *mairie,* and no one would divulge your whereabouts."

"*Mal de tête.*" The bottle of aspirin sat in clear view. "You wish something?"

"Yes, actually." She walked ahead of him into the living room and seated herself in his armchair. Her shorts were tight and rode up her thighs (their crisscrossing blue veins reminded him of a navigational chart). "*Monsieur le Maire,*" she went on, her French an offense in itself, "I've come on behalf of Hedy—Hedy Rhodes? She's in an awful bind. You must help her."

"What is the matter?"

"It's Cecil, the cad. Not only does he run off and leave her, just like that—" She snapped her gaudy fingers. "Now, Hedy finds out that all those business trips he used to take were actually golf holidays, high end. He put them on a credit card. Tens of thousands of pounds."

"*Alors?*"

"*Alors*, to pay them off he took out a loan—and what do you think he used as collateral?"

Lionel had no intention of playing guessing games.

"*Maison Joyeuse!*" she erupted. "It's mortgaged to hell, and the creditors want to put Hedy out on the street."

"She has another home, *non?* In England."

"Of course, she has another home. That's not the point. Hedy is one of Beautemps' pioneers, don't forget. She's done a great deal for this community."

"Debts must be paid, Madame Griffith." Any rational person knows this, but Hedy's friend looked at him as if he had spoken Greek. Her protruding eyes made him think of barnacles. "Terms, however, can be—how do you say?—commodious. One negotiates."

"Oh, would you? Hedy's hardly at her best right now."

"I could make inquiries, if you wish."

She bounced to her feet. "Kind of you to offer. Russ and I are off. We leave the matter in your capable hands."

"I can't promise anything."

"Right. Well, getting a little nippy, isn't it?"

Lionel saw her to the door, where she adjusted the crotch of her shorts and wished him a good winter. As she walked away his eyes gravitated on reflex to her derriere, which flattish and low-slung, had a distinctly Anglo-Saxon gravity about it. He looked away. Laura would be home soon. It was time to get started on dinner, but his headache had returned and with it a gnawing malaise. Something of the Englishwoman lingered in the room, not a smell exactly but an aura, a hint of doom. Opening the casements he waved it off. He wanted all trace of her gone.

DAVID AND MIRIAM SET OUT FOR HOME

When the day arrived to depart Beautemps, David meandered through the *Vie Dorée* searching for something, but not knowing what—a reason to stay? A reason to go? Anything would have been better than the dim sense of annulment that dogged him from room to room. It was as perfect a day as ever he'd seen. The French have a name for it: *une têmpete de ciel bleu.* Against such an onslaught of splendor his volition could not long hold. He made in haste for the staircase.

"Ready, Mum?" he called, and too edgy to wait for a response, bounded up the steps.

Miriam emerged from her bedroom dressed in a print silk dress with her silver hair tucked neatly beneath an Ascot hat, looking every inch a queen. Bearing herself with brittle dignity, she held out her arm and allowed him to escort her down the staircase. As they reached bottom she turned to inspect him.

"Head up, shoulders back."

He gathered the few things he had prepared for the drive north—a Michelin guide, a handful of CDs—and again took his mother's arm. She craned to look at him, her face crinkled into a sad smile.

"We've come through worse, *boychikal.*"

"What did you say?"

"*Nu?*" Arms akimbo she stood transformed into Miriam Cohen, the Jewish mother David had briefly known. "Don't you listen to your *mamala?*"

He would have liked to answer in this private language

smuggled through the generations in lullabies and endearments, but it had bypassed him. His native English would never suffice to return her love.

They walked through the drawing room into the foyer, and Miriam paused before the window. "This view reminds me of somewhere. Funny, I hadn't noticed it before."

"I won't miss this place."

"Give yourself time. One day you'll wake up and remember the moments, moments more precious for the hurts that came after. That really is a lovely view."

He opened the front door and maneuvered Miriam through it; like generals surrendering a fort, they marched to the Volvo. Though David had promised himself not to look back, he did. The chateau glistened like some impossible dream, an El Dorado, a Shambhala, tethered to the earth only by the unbroken blueness. His beloved pile of stones.

"Let's not dally," urged Miriam.

He started the engine, wound down the driveway, and closed the wrought iron gate behind them for the last time. As they drove through town to the asphalt road neither of them spoke. A trickle of traffic accompanied them, no one they knew. And then David saw him: Lionel, waiting beside the road where it met the river. Lionel, his battered yachting cap in hand.

Another moment and David would pass him—the distance that separated them was nothing at all, a rubbed-out dash of white line. The Frenchman stood statue still. They came alongside each other locked in a stare; the car carried David past him at a crawl. Cursing his pride David gave a long toot of the horn, and Lionel's cap bolted into the air. Again David hit the horn and watched in the rearview mirror as Lionel waved the sorry old hat in farewell. Too soon the road hair-pinned and David lost sight of his friend. There were only mulberry trees, then crosses, and finally nothing but road. As he pressed his foot to the accelerator, the way widened.

LA VIE DORÉE

The realtor planted an *Á Vendre* sign at the foot of the *Vie Dorée's* majestic mount. The last apricots went unsavored. The chateau's golden stones may have glowed golden still, but Lionel couldn't pass by without thinking of David—their jokes, the confidences they shared—and feeling the weight of those walls press down, press down like the fist of reckoning.

LIONEL DRINKS ALONE

Leftovers figure prominently in Lionel's diet of late. This afternoon's menu: day-old poached salmon and green beans, a meal he will eat alone with a newspaper propped against the wine bottle. *Vin ordinaire*, which fits the sort of day he is having.

His wife has been traveling. In the capital recently for a conference, she thought she saw Rashid Hamadi loitering on a street corner with a filterless cigarette clamped between his lips, a leather cap covering his head, and piercings along one brow. He looked unnaturally alert, as if the city had shot him full of adrenaline. She walked up to speak to him.

"*Bonjour*, Rashid. What a coincidence, our meeting like this."

"What are you doing here?" he asked without preamble.

At close range the iron studs rimming his eye resembled thorns. He wore his cap with the brim facing backward, leaving the studs to glint in the sunlight. "Research for my job. My hotel is just across the street. I couldn't very well pass by without saying hello."

"You here to rat me out?"

Thinking she had misheard, she stepped in closer and asked, "*Pardon?*"

"I'm not bothering anyone. I'm not making trouble."

"No one said you were."

"You won't tell David?" His hostility had melted, and an all-enveloping glumness taken its place.

"The Crowns have been worried sick about you. They'll be relieved to hear you're all right—you are all right, *n'est-ce pas?*" Without thinking she reached up and smoothed back his tangle of black hair, as she had often done to her own son. Their eyes met. Rashid's hands darted inside her blazer and along her breasts.

"You alone in that hotel room?" he whispered."

She had wanted to slap his face, but there was something pathetic about the boy with his mutilated face and lonely machismo. In the end she had simply walked away, leaving him as she had found him. But Lionel's anger lingered. More than once he set off for the city meaning to teach the punk a lesson, to bloody his nose, but each time he would turn the car around and head home. It was Laura he wanted, not revenge. It had always been Laura.

ROWENA CLOSES THE DISTANCE

David has made a fresh start in the Cotswolds, a place that conjures images of tea roses and cottages, the comingled scents of Stilton and lemon wax. Rowena has marked the area in her pocket atlas and for the past week has been closing in, stopping at the university towns on the pretense of salvaging her book. The libraries along the way are musty and dark. She can barely turn a page. She thumbs bindings and pictures David in a crisp Oxford shirt.

He's not expecting her. For all he knows, she might be

floating down the Nile or scaling Kilimanjaro. She told him she needed to travel, but wanderlust gave out the moment he dropped her at the airport and she watched his tidy back recede down a fluorescent corridor, then a maze of corridors. She had forgotten how it felt to be alone. One by one the planes left without her. She nearly phoned him at the chateau—he and Miriam weren't due to go north for another few days—but instead she hefted her pack onto a shoulder, hailed a taxi, and checked into the nearest hostel. The next morning she boarded a train for Nîmes, where on impulse she stopped at an Internet café and emailed David an abbreviated itinerary.

Since leaving Beautemps she has not slept on a bed wider than her hipbones, hasn't eaten a meal sitting down, has enjoyed no perch softer than a park bench, yet she can't say she misses the *Vie Dorée*. It dwarfed her. It would have dwarfed a whale. She could have lived in a single one of its closets, if its ghosts had been willing to vacate. But they held on, held on, and now the chateau is theirs.

David's last email said little, except that his mother was well and happy to be back among her grandchildren and King Charles spaniels.

If her calendar is correct, today is his birthday, his fiftieth. How awfully old. Though she is no more than a bus ride away, she won't go to him—not today. His family will probably throw a party—champagne, streamers, a ten-piece band... Better to hover near, unseen and unexpected.

England lumbers under a permanent cloud. After France, it feels as if a light has been switched off. Only the green saves it, a palette of greens, lavished along every road and footpath. When she is not haunting the libraries, she walks and pictures David shaving in his jockey shorts or pruning hedges or craning his head to follow the flight of a hawk. The images come in no particular sequence. They flash as if projected onto a screen and then quickly fade. She has forgotten how to be alone. Even the dogs put their noses to the ground as they pass her by.

Maybe tomorrow she will go to him—the party should be over by then, calm restored. She'll put on her one unwrinkled dress and stash her backpack in a locker somewhere. What's the sense of prolonging this wandering exile, this long-distance mating dance? She has only to say, I'm sorry. She has only to open wide her arms for all the lights to come back on.

DAVID STRADDLES THE WALL

It's a mild if colorless day in late September, and the sky might be a blank sheet of newsprint. David is seated behind his cottage on a low stone wall overlooking other walls, a sprawling masonry grid. Summer's remnants blow about his ankles—dying roses, stray bits of mulch. He moved here only a week ago, yet already the place feels familiar, a tad precious. He must stifle a yawn. His neighbors have yet to show themselves, though he has heard their late model Jags and Mercs purr along the lane as they come and go. The village he shall not name—what for? It is not Beautemps. He has come for the distance and nothing more.

Today is his birthday, a pesky milestone. Time to reflect, people tell him, to settle accounts and move forward. By choice he is spending the day alone, alone with a bottle of Lafitte *premier cru*, compliments of Lionel Olivier.

He could swear there's a genie in the bottle; the wine does not make him drunk. To the contrary, with each sip he finds himself more lucid. For the first time in weeks he can look back and discern, if not a grand design, at least a vague desire underpinning the events of the past year, a desire that is with him still. He doesn't attempt to name it, is content to feel it swell like a sponge in the space between his ribs, to hold it there.

Rowena's small library nestles in his den, which lined with bookcases holds his own as well. She would like this room, this house, though the chances of her passing his way are nil. No doubt she will follow the sun—Bali, Ibiza, Istanbul…? Somewhere sunny, exotic, she had said. Her skin will keep its blush. Yet he thinks she would like it here, the scale of things, and when it poured down rain, he would make a fire.

LIONEL COLLECTS HIS MAIL

A letter from David Crown, the first since his departure. If Lionel overlooks its scantily masked nostalgia, a certain buoyancy shines through. David plans to work with youth in some capacity, though the ways and means have yet to be finessed. In the meantime, he is having another go at gardening, wisely on a smaller scale. All this compressed into a single paragraph.

Questions fill the remaining pages: How are Laura and the children? Has Madame Fermat found new employment? Has Lionel chosen a new chess partner..?

Not until the last few lines does David's real concern surface: Rashid Hamadi. Can Lionel please have him located? More precisely, can he help David force his beneficence upon him? The boy has not been in touch with him and David fears the worst—another knifing, another stint in prison… Poor David, having to drag through life a conscience the size of a lost empire! Lionel suspects this is an English malady, for in retrospect he sees David as devoutly English (whatever else he may be), more, not less, English than the Rhodes or Windsors. The young Hamadi will have his revenge. By refusing to take, he will bring his faithful supporter to his knees.

Lionel will dash off a letter to his friend from home this evening, advising David to leave the wily ex-con to him and get on with his plans. Laura's encounter he does not mention, cannot mention without feeling a still-simmering anger take him by the throat. Let the Hamadies of the world steer clear of Beautemps, where men do not covet their neighbor's wife and no one goes hungry.

He will tell David to keep his eye on the future, to lead the young there with his inimitable mixture of zest and sobriety. But he must begin *now*. His children's generation races toward oblivion. They dream in euros, max out their credit cards—what's to stop them? The time bomb of global warming is their only certainty. And whom but their parents do they have to thank, the same wizened stooges who now stand on the sidelines waving flags, urging faith. If Lionel's own holds, if the night bombards him with stars, he will, perhaps, venture a postscript: Come back to us one day, David Crown. *Reviens, non?*

DAVID LANDS ON HIS FEET

Four o'clock and still David is glued to this wall, the bottle not quite empty, his backside half frozen. He would walk to the house for a jacket, but his work here is not yet done. He will not get up, absolutely not, until he can stand amidst the dying roses of his garden and belt out with ear-splitting sincerity, *"Je ne regrette rien! C'est payé, balayé, oublié..."* To go forward without regret—is this not the toughest task a man can set himself? *"Mes chagrins, mes plaisirs, je n'ai plus besoin d'eux..."* No use indeed. He opens his arms as if to embrace the landscape's boxy symmetry, noting as he does so that the lawn needs cutting. *"Je ne regrette rien!"*

But he's not in voice. No, he's gone thick about the tongue. The neighbor peers at him through her net curtains; he can't make out her face, only the broadish outline of her torso as she fades right. Too late he raises his glass. The genie has left the bottle and is turning backward somersaults along an invisible tightrope.

Torn between resolve and the first twinges of a stomach upset, David slides from the wall and lands with a thud on his two numb feet. The empty bottle follows.

The light has fled; cold knocks at David's bones. In a moment he will go for a jacket, put on the kettle, but someone is walking toward him, a figure familiar even in outline.

"Is that you, Barry?"

His brother raises a hand in greeting. "You don't mind, do you?" He looks sheepish. "I couldn't *not* come."

"Don't be silly—cup of tea?"

"Later. What have you been about, anyway? All rosy-cheeked you are."

"Just getting some air." David hooks an arm through his brother's and they set off for the cottage.

Barry eyes the bottle. "Don't suppose this has anything to do with it?" David studies his own feet, thinking he might eyeball them into a straight line. "Relax, I'm not some schoolmaster catching you out. Wouldn't mind a glass myself, actually."

David gives the bottle a discreet shake. "I'll open another."

"Joanne and the girls send regards. They think France has made an eccentric of you, but never mind. Nothing wrong with a bit of solitude."

"I've never been one for parties."

They enter the conservatory, switch on a light, and wend their way through the havoc of odds and ends en route to the kitchen. David fiddles with a corkscrew until Barry relieves him of it. "Sorry, old habit," he says. "I'll get a glass—where are they?"

David looks at the packing boxes and shrugs. "Heck, we'll drink from the bottle."

They gravitate toward a bay window overlooking the garden.

"Getting dark already," he murmurs, searching the slate gray sky for a first star. "I've crossed over."

"Into what?"

"Old age, I suppose."

"Don't believe it, kiddo. Hair or no hair, you're still the lad."

They pass the bottle in silence for a few minutes then clear a place to perch. Barry unbuttons his trench coat and is about to drape it atop a shrouded column. "What's this?" he says and lifts its drop-cloth cover, revealing the face of a grandfather clock. "How Dad used to love this old piece of junk. Dig it out of a closet?"

"My only memento."

"Got it in Poland, of all places. Who would have expected Willy Crown to take his one vacation in his ancestral home?"

David shakes his head. "I had always thought of him as the man who never looked back."

"He got sentimental in his old age, sank a chunk of cash in renovating a synagogue in Lodz."

"A synagogue? I didn't think Willy would ever set foot in one."

"This one had a history. Our great grandfather had his bar mitzvah there."

"Willy never spoke of it—why not? Why couldn't he let his own son know him?"

A roll of thunder swallows up his brother's reply.

Waving away the bottle, Barry bolts to his feet. "Hurry, before it pours. I've got something for you in the Rover."

"Let me get a torch."

They collide at the front door and step out into a night for one fleeting moment luminous, raining down light. David looks up, not blinded but dazzled, a man given a taste of immortality worth the half century it has cost him.

Barry de-activates the burglar alarm by remote and then lifts the hatch. David directs the beam inside. "What is it?"

"A drum set: snare, bass, cymbals… the whole shmeer. Thought you might want to bang something around, make some noise."

"Let loose."

The first raindrops catch his brother full in the face. "Yeah, let loose. Isn't it about time?"

A Funeral

Rashid Hamadi's mother has died of pneumonia, a corpse at thirty-six. Having closed Rashid's file and lost track of the boy's whereabouts, Lebrun calls Lionel with the news.

"What am I supposed to do about it?" Lionel's anger reignites, a rawness that runs through him like a pike.

"Just thought you'd want to know, if not for the kid then for Crown."

"For once you're right."

"No, for once *you're* right. You old pussy."

Relieved to be done with Lebrun, Lionel hangs up the phone. The task of finding the young Hamadi could take all day. He calls his secretary, leaves a note for his wife, and checks the motor oil. Ten minutes later, he is driving down the highway toward the city with the radio on and Jacques Chirac ranting about OPEC and the rising price of oil. The sunflowers have been decapitated, he notices. Soon the fields will be one brown monotone.

He switches off the radio, wills his mind blank, and drives.

The city is a magnet for unemployed teenagers—pierced, tattooed, jockeying for spare change. Lionel slowly cruises the streets beginning at the center and working outward toward the *banlieues*, where the walls lean dark with graffiti and litter blows through the gutters. He circles, doubles back. Rashid leans against a storefront—no mistaking the leather cap, the ribby torso. The boy, inert as a paving stone, watches him drive past without the least expression.

Lionel parks at a distance, angling for the boy's blind spot, and approaches only close enough to make himself heard. "Bad news, about your mother." A greeting is more than he can muster.

"A *pol* can only be bad news."

"Look, Hamadi, I'm in no mood for your impudence. Your mother has died. The funeral has been arranged. Tomorrow."

A stream of pedestrians passes between them. Lionel steps in closer.

"Does my brother know?" the boy asks.

"Lebrun's on his way there now."

"Almighty Lebrun."

It takes all of Lionel's self-possession not to slap the boy's face. "How will you get home for the funeral?"

"Home? Who says I'm going home?"

"Think of your father. He shouldn't be alone at a time like this."

"I don't suppose the old cheapskate has sent bus fare?" He steps away from the wall and upturns his empty palms. "*Pas de fric*, dude." He picks up a battered knapsack, army surplus, and begins to walk away.

"Hold it right there! I'm taking you back to Beautemps. Get in the car."

The boy veers and backhands Lionel across the chest, not hard—he's no heavyweight—but with enough pluck to put the older man on guard. "What's with you, *eh*? *Eh*?" You want to fight? Fine, let's fight." Lionel returns the blow in kind and watches the color rise on Rashid's skinny neck.

"Piss off, Olivier. I'm a minor. There's a law."

"What you are is a delinquent. If it weren't for David Crown, you'd be back in the slammer."

"So this isn't about your wife's tits?"

Lionel hits him again, harder and across the mouth. *"Tais-toi!* Don't you dare speak my wife's name. Don't! I won't tolerate it."

"Du calme, mon ami."

"Mon ami, nothing. Your one friend was David Crown, and you ran him off."

"The *mec* left. He didn't belong and he knew it."

"If you hadn't assaulted him…"

"If you think so little of me, why didn't you let me drown?"

"Have you any idea all David did for the village? The war memorial park—blank check. The improvements to the square—blank check. The fireworks for the independence day celebration—"

"Does he ask about me?"

Lionel's fists unclench. He feels an urge to take Rashid by the hand and walk with him in the open air. The boy's so bony, so utterly alone. "David asks about you in every letter."

It isn't the response the boy expects, and he almost smiles.

"What do you say we have some lunch?" Lionel can see him salivate. "You're on the street, aren't you?"

Rashid nods and his audacious façade falls away.

"About Madame Olivier… I didn't mean her any disrespect. She pointed out the hotel and stroked my hair and—what do I know? I've never been with a woman."

"You'll learn."

"And now I don't have a mother." His voice catches; he turns away.

Lionel hands the boy a handkerchief and steps to the other end of the sidewalk, pretending to study the road signs.

"Can you get me to the funeral, Monsieur Olivier? I'll pay you back."

"After lunch."

They walk a short distance to a pizzeria and take a table near a fluorescent fish tank. A waitress with one short leg and one long writes down their order and hobbles, whistling, to the kitchen.

"I've got a proposition for you," Lionel says, trying to sound nonchalant. "There's a Dutch farmer in Beautemps who could use a hand. Swijdendorp is his name. I've spoken to him about you and he has agreed to let you stay with him in exchange for help with his land—he keeps a few cows, grows some truffles. You can finish school, think about what comes next."

"Whose idea was this?"

"My wife's, of course."

The pizza arrives and they eat with silent gusto, having taken each other's measure and made their peace. When not a crust remains, Lionel wipes his hands on a serviette and extends the right across the sauce-spattered table.

"Do we have a deal?"

"You probably think I'm an asshole." He uses the English term, *asshole*, and his accent isn't half bad. "Sure mister, sure."

They shake hands, Rashid inscrutable behind his grid of scars, and Lionel relieved to have done right, not only by society but by David Crown, whose karmic presence he feels in the fluid opalescence of the aquarium.

He gets up, shoulders Rashid's knapsack, and steers the boy by an elbow toward his parked car. Rashid's ribs poke through his threadbare tee shirt. Seated at last in the passenger seat, the boy, looking younger in profile, unscathed and unguarded, yawns and nestles into the leather upholstery. Lionel would like to tell him that mistakes can be forgiven, that memory can be kind, but instead he switches on the radio and drives. There will be time enough for words once the city is behind them.

EROS ETERNAL

At seven forty-five Laura lets herself in, sets down her latchkey and her briefcase, and crosses to Lionel's armchair, where she greets him with a pinch and settles onto his lap. "*Ça va, Capitaine?*"

There seems too much to say to say anything at all, so Lionel only presses his cheek to her breast and growls.

"I know, *chéri*. I know."

They remain like this for—how long?—with a breeze coming in the window and Laura's hair lifting from her shoulders to caress his cheek.

"Hear anything from the children?" he asks and she fills him in on their latest academic coups, *bons mots*, and heartthrobs. Two years away from home and already they are less his.

As if intuiting his thoughts she chides, "But we have our own lives."

Lives that have grown fuller, at a cost. How rare, how worth preserving, the unscheduled moment *à deux*. Sinking deeper into the upholstery, they resume silence, and the bells strike eight and eight again.

His wife opens the window wider. The cicadas *churr*, the river laughs, and the moon, slow to rise, casts its amber glow into the room. Laura lifts her face to the breeze. "I gave Foussier notice today." Lionel is delighted and she knows it, though he takes pains to contain his joy. "Teaching is what matters. I think I'll reapply for next term."

"*Comme tu veux, Matelot.*"

Slipping from his clasp, she rises and pulls him to his feet.

"Dinner?" he says mechanically.

She hooks a clutch of tender fingers into the waistband of his pants and gazes toward the staircase, hardly a subtle gesture. What man would think to resist? Appetizers *à l' horizontal* with dessert still to savor. Life is a banquet, make no mistake: wine, lust, love, a harvest of fruits, a harvest of hearts… Eros, whatever her season, can only be a profligate.

"It's been a long summer," Laura says, reading his thoughts only to wash them away like a quenching white wave.

RETREAT

Malta, Marrakech, Timbuktu? It's not the miles that separate them but an inner distance, the heart's retreat. Tomorrow David will pack Rowena's books and store them in the attic, if only to spare himself the temptation to finger their bindings.

WHAT REMAINS

Dear Rashid,

I am posting this letter to Lionel in the hope that he will forward it to you, wherever you may be.

Did I fail you, my friend? I have been hoping every day since your departure for a chance to speak with you of things that have been weighing on my heart (yes, I do have one). Distance has helped me place the events of this past summer in perspective. I may never know why I was singled out to witness a hate crime (such grand panjandrums may be beyond human comprehension), but my feelings about you, for you, are clear. When all the big questions and bright ideals fall away, affection is all that is left.

So, my dear *copain*, my *habibi*, wherever these words find you, please know that you are never out of mind. A part of you has stayed behind in every shared poem—Lawrence would have understood this alchemy, I think. But as I scavenge my shelved verses for a scrap of grace, it is gentle Yeats who whispers:

"I have spread my dreams under your feet;

Tread softly because you tread on my dreams."

I will leave off here, lest I begin quoting Emily Dickinson.

Always,
David

ROWENA'S CHOICE

Rowena has had a nervous collapse, they tell her. It's all very *Carry On Nurse:* the hospital ward with its rows of iron beds, the shuttling of trays and bedpans, that blend of blood and gore and stoic good humor that makes mortality entertaining. How she came to be here, she doesn't know. Amnesia, they say. The past and present don't meet up: One minute she's sitting down in a pub with a fizzy water on the table in front of her, and the next crashing through the stratosphere with a hollow where her mind once was. She can put no names to faces; the faces themselves blur into anonymity as she probes them. And yet the void they form is benign. She feels no pain.

A pale intern in scrubs approaches with a rubberducky expression. "Right. We've checked your vitals and given you a little something to help you relax. Have a lie-down and you should be fine."

"I'm sleepy."

"Right. Well, who shall we call then?"

Rowena's mother, who will weep and recite Hail Mary's and find some way, however unfounded, to blame herself? Her friend Anne at the library, to whom she has not written since leaving Maine and who will not in any case have the faintest idea what to do? There is only David—solid, reliable David—who has been waiting for his chance to be her hero from the day they met.

"There's no one," Rowena tells the doctor.

He frowns and scribbles a note on her chart. On his way out, he confers with a male nurse who adds a scribble of his own before planting himself at the foot of the bed to peer at her over the wire rims of his bifocals. "Here all alone, lass? What are we going to do with you? Can't very well put you out on the street, can we?"

"A hotel, any hotel, will be fine."

"There was a young lady in to see you earlier; looked like a vampire but seemed a decent sort. Left her number, in case you needed anything."

"I don't know any vampires… from the pub, maybe?"

"I'll ring her up."

Rowena says nothing, only yawns and lies back in the curious void. She must doze, for when she again gazes toward the foot of her bed a young woman in clingy pants has displaced the male nurse. She chews gum. "Awake, luv?" she says in a voice too loud for the hour. "Let's get you out of here. Chop-chop." Then thinking better of it, "I'll just hijack the nurse."

Some time later, having dressed and arranged to settle her bill, Rowena follows the woman to a dented Mini and allows herself to be driven to a row house whose front garden has been paved over to accommodate the car. Her name is Jasmine, she tells Rowena, and she shares the house with a psychopath and three cats. All the lights are out by the time they arrive and they tiptoe to Jasmine's room and close the door.

"Hot water bottle?" she offers.

"Don't bother."

The room holds only one bed. "You don't fancy girls, do you?" Jasmine says, stripping down to her underthings, which are red and abbreviated. "Because I don't."

"That's settled."

They arrange themselves beneath the duvet (the cats stretch out on top), and Jasmine flops onto her side, facing Rowena, and gives a low whistle. "Has anyone ever told you you're flipping crazy?" She laughs like water going down the drain and punches her guest on the arm. "That wanker who kept trying to chat you up, you demolished him, full stop. Needs castrating, that one."

"I don't remember."

"Well, let me tell you, you were brilliant." Jasmine rolls onto her back dislodging the smallest and most skittish of the cats. "Sorry, Dolly," she says and lies still. "Don't see many Yanks here this time of year."

Rowena waits for her hostess to call her a peculiar bird, but she only chews her cuticles.

"You work?"

"Leave of absence."

"Work sucks. I think about becoming an escort but now with all the stuff going around—not that it stops anyone. Men are only interested in your parts, anyway."

"Not all men." Rowena is thinking of David and the

kicked look he got when she told him she needed to go. 'But this is so sudden,' he said and choked up, able to say no more.

Jasmine, reaching over her, flicks a button on the clock radio. "You have a boyfriend, sounds like."

"Sort of."

"Then why aren't you with him?"

"Because I've done something he will never forgive."

"That bad, *eh?*" she says and goes silent. Just when Rowena thinks she has fallen asleep, she feels the woman's fist nudge her elbow. "Well, luv, you don't have to tell him."

◆

But Rowena needs to tell someone, a stranger maybe or the demons inside her head.

It was a brisk day, stunning in its clarity, and she had wanted to spend it outdoors moving through the landscape she had come to love. Humming, she set out along Beautemps' wooded perimeter. The route had become her turf, the boundary points she daily marked with the tread of her sandals. Unlike most afternoons, patches of cloud blocked the sun at intervals. At those times a pedestrian could almost feel autumn giving notice, waiting to descend.

She turned back toward the chateau and followed the track that led past Arjen's farm. She had no intention of stopping; enough had already been said. She remembers dogs barking, the gate creaking as it swung back and forth on rusted hinges, the sun suddenly locked away in a bank of clouds.

She looked for Arjen's truffle dogs and saw them tethered to a fencepost. It was not like the farmer to leave the dogs tied in full sunlight in the heat of the day. Their panting and whimpering made her stop and look around. Not a soul in sight. Wracked by pity, she tore at the rope binding the dogs until its knots loosened. Moving as one, the dogs broke free and raced, furiously barking, toward the farmhouse.

Rowena followed at a distance, walking through the gate and along the perimeter of Aryen's meticulously tended crop rows. Midway, she heard a cry, ear-splitting, barely human. There were tools—a screwdriver, a chisel—scattered on the ground nearby—and beyond them a prone body.

And then the nightmare came into focus: Arjen, wild-eyed, curled round himself like a snail, and at a distance of several feet Cecil Rhodes, splay-legged, facedown in the dust.

"*Mijn God, wat heb ik gedaan? Wat heb ik gedaan?*"

She stopped and crouched alongside, but the farmer seemed not to see her. "Arjen? What has happened?"

He uncurled slightly and she saw that his shirtfront was stained red and brown, several shades of these colors, one overlapping the other. "I told him I didn't want trouble—it was him. He came at me. *Mijn God*, I'll lose everything, everything…"

"There was a fight?"

"I don't fight. I don't believe in that shit. He kept pushing me, pushing me, then he got hold of the sledgehammer. *Godver. Wat nu?* I'll lose everything."

She gestured toward Cecil, aware suddenly of the blood drying on his Hawaiian shirt. "Is he… dead?"

Arjen upturned his palms. "The dogs. The dogs did it. They got loose somehow."

She might have confessed, might have taken the guilt upon herself, but would the truth have spared Arjen his farm, his freedom? She had read enough courtroom dramas to know that things like chance or karma have little influence on the outcome of a trial. Arjen had a motive, the prosecutor would argue, he was younger than Cecil, bigger, his dogs had been trained to kill, he had only to give the command.

The farmer began again to whimper.

"Get a grip. We need to turn him over." She walked

over to Cecil, knelt, and wedged the heel of her hand beneath one of his hipbones. "Hurry up," she snapped, "get his other side."

He did as she said and Cecil's broad, flabby body flopped onto its back. His eyes, half lidded, shone with blood. There was blood on his collar, his pant legs, though not as much as she would have expected. In two or three places she could see tooth marks. She bent lower and placed her ear to his lips. "Nothing. He's gone."

"*Mijn God, wat—*"

"Shut up and think. We've got to get him out of here." She reached into the pockets of Cecil's soiled shorts and removed a wadded handkerchief, a billfold, and an inhaler of the type used by asthmatics. "He must have had a respiratory problem. Or his heart gave out."

The farmer turned green.

"Get a shovel," she heard herself whisper.

He hesitated a moment then rose, swaying, to his feet and walked haltingly to his work shed. The dogs barked and shoved their noses into the dead man's groin. She looked away. Moments later, Arjen was back with a rusted garden spade quaking in his hands.

"You know what you need to do."

He said nothing, only hung his ponderous head against his breastbone.

"Hide him—bury him."

"I was digging a root cellar…" He pointed in the direction of the kitchen garden.

"Okay then, I'll wait for you over there. Give a sign when you're ready."

His sweating hand clutched at the fabric of her tee shirt. "I can't."

"What choice do you have?"

He extended the spade toward her. "Please."

"If you can't do it, what makes you think I can?"

"Please."

"For God's sake don't ask me. Don't even ask."

"I have no right, no guts. You always saw through me. I wasn't man enough to win you away from Crown, and I'm not man enough to save myself. I'll lose everything."

They dragged Cecil's body to the hole intended for the cellar and there the farmer's strength, if strength it could be called, gave out.

"Give me the shovel." She heaved earth upon the corpse, knowing that with each shovelful she was burying her own future, her "golden life." Cecil Rhodes, whom even now she can do no more than pity, had, with his spite and his rage, doomed her.

When the hole was full, she clapped the dirt from her hands and turned to go.

"Wait." The farmer darted into the house and returned with a dampened washcloth, which he ran over Rowena's face and hands and the front of her shirt. "You look all right. You're all right."

"Not really, Arjen. I think I've done something terribly wrong."

The farmer's hands reached out, stopping just short of her shoulders. "For me—you did it for me."

◆

Rowena lies awake listening to Jasmine's shallow snoring, its tempo as even as a ticking clock. At her feet, purring, the trio of cats. Beyond the window the occasional belch of diesel. Oddly at ease in this borrowed domesticity, she can look back without panic or regret, with little feeling at all. Every image she calls to mind is picture-perfect: the hillside on fire with poppies, the fields expiring in sunflowers, the golden chateau an invitation to dream. A setting in search of an idyll. How the Duke must have hated to die!

At her center she is empty, light. When the doctor sedated her, he took away the dread she has lived with these past weeks, leaving her in a state that might almost be innocence. She is ready now to face David and let his storm blue eyes roll over her like Judgment. Ready to speak the words, "There are things a woman must do sometimes. *Private* things."

Jasmine has set the radio for seven, but Rowena will be gone by then. Dawn will find her on David's doorstep, more air than flesh but hoping still. So much left at halves, the high carved bed still breathing his scent. Her books he can keep, she wants only to talk—shouldn't lovers know each other before they part? What makes people hate she is no closer to grasping, but love she just may be beginning to understand.

MIDNIGHT

The night has turned blustery, a contest of sighs. The cottage's warped casements invite the wind indoors. Moving dust makes nebulae of the lamplight. That the house is haunted, that David will share it with ghosts both known and yet to be encountered, he accepts without complaint. The past doesn't faze him anymore.

Not quite steady on his feet he takes a lacquered box from a cardboard crate and a small metallic object, still wrapped in a sheet of Lionel's monogrammed stationery, from the box. From another crate he takes a hammer and a plastic bag of tacks. Stepping out onto the front landing, taking aim, he nails the mezuzah to the doorpost. An act as old as Leviticus. Why, then, does his hand waver? Whether the uppermost pole should lean left or right he can't be certain, but lean it must. At this juncture, even the heavens are off plumb. Midnight has come and he is drunk at last, but not drunk enough for mythic visions or facile pronouncements about the meaning of life. As if fifty years were time enough to puzzle it out. As if life could be other than dreamed.

David reenters the house and weaves among his shrouded furnishings and packing boxes, searching for a bed. He knows there will be one and that some day—soon, he thinks—he will not be alone in it. If this is faith, then count him a believer. But first, sleep. To sleep…

Acknowledgments

Shortly after the events of 9/11, my then partner and I considered making France a second home. We had always enjoyed French *joie de vivre* and gotten on well with the people we met on our numerous sojourns in the country. We knew from newspaper accounts that France had suffered a spike in hate crimes but found it difficult to reconcile such headlines with the bonhomie we encountered throughout placid, village France.

For their invaluable help with the nuances of French language and culture, I thank cyber-angels Serge Villa and Claudine Lair. Thanks also to British expat Sue Baker, whose cottage in the Dordogne provided an ideal window on a village very much like Beautemps.

Where would I be without Beta-readers David Liss and Adam Sydney, whose discernment and keen eye for detail keep me humble?

A toast to my cheering section: Laurence and Marilyn Shames, Jeannine Relly, Alice Pringle, Vera Marie Badertscher, Ginia Desmond, Eric and Jane Force, Rusty and Marilyn Shteir, Arlene Kellman, Lori Fraesdorf, David Gunzberg-Frank, Aryen Hart, Shay Salomon, Kasia Yuzka, Georgia Reed and others dear to my heart whom I promise to include by name next book.

And finally, warm thanks to the French for their hospitality, good taste, and good sense. *Echo Year* is a love letter to people of goodwill who dare to reach across the divide of hatred. May we learn both from history's light and dark chapters and go forward in the purest spirit of *Liberté, Egalité, Fraternité!*